ROCK 'N' ROLL PRINCESSES WEAR BLACK

By Kelly Polark

Reading rocks!

♡ Kelly Polark

Big Smile Press, LLC

Copyright 2014 by Kelly Polark
BIG SMILE PRESS, LLC

ISBN-13: 978-0988846227
ISBN-10: 0988846225

Cover Design by Steven Novak
Cover photography by Tom Maple

This book is for my mom,
Trudy, and my sister, Denise.

Thank you for forcing me
to listen to the rock 'n' roll
radio station before school.

♬

STOP BY AND SAY
"HEY!" ONLINE!

You can find Kelly Polark
all over the web.
Facebook:
facebook.com/AuthorKellyPolark
Twitter:
www.twitter.com/kellypolark
Her writing blog:
www.kpolark.blogspot.com
Her celebrity book
recommendation site:
www.bookrecsthatrock.blogspot.com
And at Intrepid Publications:
www.intrepidpublications.com

Chapter One

My mom coined our place, *The Loud House*.

"Yes, I'm back in black!" blasted from the family room speakers. My little brother cried like a baby in his bedroom, because, well, he's a baby. I stepped into my room and shut the door for some rare peace and quiet. Why couldn't our place be *The Occasionally Loud House*?

Even with my door closed, I could hear my dad listening to his AC/DC playlist on the iPod speakers. He always did that when he paid bills. AC/DC is a *classic* rock band. Which means they're old. I like music and all. In fact, I love it. But there's a time for rocking out, and there's a time to get things done. I desperately needed to find something to wear to Brooke's birthday party. Right now. Stat. Immediately. Pronto. If only my brother would go back to sleep. He should be napping now. He usually can sleep through music playing, dogs barking, anything in *The Loud House*. Mom said that he's teething. Another reason for my parents to smother him with attention. Another reason to say, "Stef, wait a minute. Stef, I can't do this now. Stef, your brother is the only thing we care about." Okay, maybe they've never said that last one, but they've probably thought it.

1

I glanced at my neon guitar clock on the wall. It was almost time to leave for Brooke's birthday party, and I was anxious to get out of the house and away from my baby brother. Brooke's party was at the roller rink. I'm not great at skating, but lots of girls in my sixth-grade class were going. It should be fun, even though it was a Pink at the Rink party. According to the invitation, we *had* to wear pink to the party. Pink! It might as well be called a Stink at the Rink Party. Black is the only cool color. It's very rock 'n' roll, and black goes with anything.

I know about rock 'n' roll because my dad is a musician. He plays guitar in a band with my cousin Gina. The band is called Quandary, because they couldn't agree on a band name. My dad is also an accountant. He calls it his day job. He says he works to live, and lives to play music. Whatever that means.

My mom called, "Stefani! It's almost time to go!" See, even my name screams rock 'n' roll. Mom named me after her favorite musician (favorite musician besides my dad, of course). Even my baby brother, Gerard, is named after a lead singer. What do you expect from a family with a dog named Lyric?

I rummaged through the black tops in my bottom drawer and finally picked out a shirt with a skull on it. Not much pink, but it would have to do. I took off my black concert tee and slipped on the

2

new one. I kept my favorite black jeans on even though they felt a little tight. I've had them since last year, but they had little silver studs on the pockets that would reflect the strobe lights at the roller rink. I brushed my hair quickly with my glittery black brush and tossed it onto my dresser. I tore down the stairs humming the Beatles "Birthday" song.

"Hey, Stef! You ready?" my mom called.

"Yep! Where's the gift?" I asked. Mom handed me the bubblegum pink gift bag. I peeked inside. A book and an iTunes gift card, Mom's standard gift. She always thinks that everyone loves music as much as she does, and that reading is the next best thing to music. Actually, most of my friends do like the gifts she picks out.

"Stefani! You aren't wearing any pink," Mom said as she smoothed my hair with the palm of her hand.

"Yes, I am," I said, and I pointed to the hot pink bow atop the skull on my shirt.

"I know you have some pink accessories somewhere," Mom said under her breath before she ran up to my room. She came down with a hot pink headband and plopped it onto my head.

"At least wear this," she scolded. "It is a pink party."

Gerard started wailing again from the bedroom.

"Simon, can you get Gerard?" Mom called to my dad.

Dad didn't answer. I looked for him in the kitchen where the music was still blaring. There was the pile of envelopes and the checkbook at the table, but no Dad.

"Dad!" I yelled. Where in the world was he? We were going to be late.

Chapter Two

"Simon!" Mom yelled again. She sighed and leapt up two stairs at a time to get to Gerard. Gerard was really screaming now.

"Darn it!" I heard her yell from upstairs. "Stef, can you come up and help me?"

I groaned and pounded up the stairs. "What?!"

"Gerard soaked through his diaper. Would you please run the tub so I can give him a quick swish before I go?"

"Mom! We have to go. Now," I complained.

"I'm not taking a urine-soaked baby into the car, and I have no idea where your dad went," Mom snapped.

"Fine." I stomped into the bathroom, ran the water and threw in a wash cloth.

I went back in Gerard's room where Mom was changing the light blue starry crib sheets. Dad wanted to have a guitar-themed nursery, but Mom thought that was a bit too mature of a theme for a newborn. They compromised on a "Star Light, Star Bright" theme. Since Gerard was their little rock star. As if to remind me that he was the favorite, naked Gerard sat up on a towel and grinned at me.

"Don't smile at me you stupid baby," I whispered to him.

"Stef!" Mom said. I guess she heard me.

"I'll be in the car waiting," I said to Mom. We were now six minutes late. I went downstairs and turned down the music. Still no Dad.

I heard Mom putting Gerard in the tub with a splash. That will be another six minutes.

I grabbed the gift bag, swung open the door to the garage and bumped into my dad.

"Hey," he said. He had a piece of grass stuck in his goatee.

"Where were you?" I asked as I plucked the stray grass off of his face.

"Ouch! Easy," Dad patted his chin. "I was just across the street. Jim got a riding lawn mower. I wanted to check it out. What's with the mad face?"

"You. Gerard. I'm late to Brooke's party," I stated through clenched teeth.

"Oh, I thought Mom was taking you," Dad said.

"Where is she?'

"Where else? With Gerard!" I climbed in the back seat and slammed the car door.

My dad hightailed it into the house. I fumed in the car until my mom came out.

"I'm sorry, hon. Let's go. Dad is rocking Gerard to sleep." She buckled her seat belt.

"So, who else is going to the party?" Mom said, acting like she didn't just majorly mess up.

I pretended I didn't hear her and stared out the window.

"Stef? Anyone else I know going to the party?"

I put on my headphones and played an angry metal song on my iPod. Mom took the hint and stopped bugging me. She turned up the radio instead and sang along to a Buckcherry song. Apparently it didn't bother her that her daughter wasn't speaking to her.

Mom used to care about how I felt. We used to always do things together, too. Cards. Movies. Actual conversations. Now she's always with Gerard. Who had kids eleven years apart anyway?! It's not like Gerard and I could ever be friends. He's a stinky little blob of a person who can't do anything. He's just a pain in my buttocks.

Chapter Three

"Okay, we're here." Mom's tired brown eyes smudged with eyeliner peered at me through the rearview mirror as she shut off the car. The parking lot of the roller rink was packed. I jumped out of the car. Mom hustled out and tried to put her arm around me, but I shrugged it off. I entered the dark foyer of the rink, and she followed. Mom informed the cashier we were there for the Pink Party, and I opened the next door to the commotion of movers and shakers. All the girls were already rolling around the rink. The lights flashed to the music. Everyone was dressed to code. It looked like someone threw up pink cotton candy on everyone. I groaned. I hated being late, and I couldn't believe I was being forced to be part of this pink explosion. Who wants to be told what to wear to a birthday party?

"Have fun, Stef. I'll be back at 3:00." Mom gave my hand a squeeze.

I said, "Okay, bye," as I looked for my friends. I squeezed her hand back. She did give me a ride after all.

"Hey Stef!" my best friend, Gabi Rivera, called to me. She was wearing a pastel pink skirt with a pink and white striped polo shirt. Her curly,

8

shoulder-length, dark brown hair was pulled back in a white headband. I had to admit, she looked cute in pink.

Gabi looked me up and down and whispered, "Stef, you could have borrowed a pink shirt from me."

I shrugged. I didn't care. I am so not a pink person. Black has always been my signature color. Then I noticed Brooke staring and pointing at me to Olivia. Olivia shook her blond head.

Brooke glided over to me on her skates. "Hi Stef! Didn't you read on the invite it was a pink party?"

I pointed to my headband, then to my pink gift.

She smiled and took my gift to the gift table. Apparently a present is a "Get Out of Pink Free" card.

"Oh, nice of you to show up, Stef," Olivia said as she followed Brooke.

"Geez! It's not my fault," I mumbled under my breath. I noticed Olivia and Brooke's matching outfits as they rolled away with their arms linked. They both wore long, shimmery hot pink tops. Olivia wore denim leggings with hers, and Brooke wore hot pink leggings with a lace trim. How cutesy.

Brooke was usually pretty nice, but Olivia could be a snot. They've been best friends since kindergarten when Olivia's family moved next door to Brooke's house, so they were a matched set. If you were friends with one, you had to hang out with the other.

I made my way through the pink crowd of girls and put my rental roller skates on. Even the laces were pink today!

I skated towards Gabi. A catchy tune from Nickelodeon came on. We linked arms following the flow of traffic, and circled the rink. Flashes of pink whizzed by me, so I took it slow. I wasn't as comfortable on skates as the rest of the girls. I started to get in a better mood as I hummed to the song. We took a few more laps, and I felt myself getting the hang of the wheels beneath me. Gabi and I even tried skating to the music.

"Look who's here!" Gabi pointed.

It was Josh, the seventh grader that used to ride our bus. He was kind of a loud mouth, but he was funny. He also played guitar at the talent show in the fall. And he was cute.

"Don't point!" I gasped and batted Gabi's hand, but then I lost my balance.

I stumbled and fell onto the cold, hard floor. Poor Gabi fell along with me. Right in front of Josh.

"Yow!" Gabi shouted as she landed on top of my ankle.

I shrieked, "Ouch!" Gabi took my hand and helped me up. She led me to the bench next to the drab gray-carpeted wall. I did not even turn around to see if Josh actually saw us fall. I really didn't want to know. But with my dumb luck, I was sure he did. I could feel my face turn as pink as Gabi's skirt.

Brooke's mom scurried over in her tall, brown leather boots to check on us.

"Are you girls okay?" she asked.

"I'm fine, but Stef hurt her ankle," Gabi replied.

"I'll go get you some ice for that, Stef," Brooke's mom said.

"Thanks," I grimaced.

Brooke's mom ran back with a baggie filled with ice. I took off my right roller skate, and gingerly placed the bag on my ankle. It was so cold that it was hard to keep it on for a long time. I avoided looking at anyone for a few minutes.

I checked to see if my ankle was bruised, but it was only rosy from the cold ice. My ankle decided to join the pink party, I guess.

My traitor ankle and I sat on the bench and watched the Pink Roller Derby roll by to the music. Josh skated swiftly by with his buddies a few times, but he didn't look my way. One friend pretended he was about to fall and laughed as they exited the roller rink onto the carpet. I wasn't sure if he was making fun of me or just being silly. I felt my ears burn at the thought anyway. Now my ears joined the pink party.

I continued to watch Josh and his two friends skate toward the arcade. Josh held his cell

11

phone and texted as he skated. Now that took talent. The friend who pretended to fall waved his dollars in front of the other guy's freckled face. He should spend that money on shampoo instead of games. He really needed his hair washed. Grease City.

"Hey, Stef!" someone yelled from the rink. I jumped out of my boy trance to see who yelled. Jenna smiled at me as Olivia dragged her by the hand across the main floor. I waved to Jenna and a few girls from our class as they skated by. Gabi sat by me for a few songs, so I wasn't too lonely.

"So, you think anyone saw us fall?" I asked Gabi.

"Uh, would you believe me if I said no?" Gabi replied.

"No," I said.

"Well, then you are smarter than Olivia looks," Gabi giggled. She could always make me laugh. Maybe laughter *is* the best medicine.

Chapter Four

Brooke's mom motioned all of us over with a graceful wave and a bright white smile. Finally it was cake time. Gabi held my arm as I hobbled over to the party room festive with pink streamers and a table loaded with pink presents and a framed photo of a smiling Brooke. She was an only child, and her parents always made sure she had the best parties and best of everything else too. Lucky girl. A huge rectangular cake with twelve pink candles and pink roses sat on the table. I don't love pink, but I do love cake. And it was my favorite -- chocolate cake with chocolate filling. Brooke's mom handed each of us a piece of cake and a mini plastic jug of milk.

"Yummy!" I said with my mouth full to Gabi. We watched Brooke open present after present. She smiled a genuine smile as she took the iTunes gift card and book out of my gift bag.

"I think I'll buy either the new Justin Bieber or Justin Timberlake album. I guess if your name is Justin, I heart you! Thanks, Stef," she giggled.

Olivia nudged me. "Hmmph. Good thing you gave her a good present. You didn't wear pink or skate at her party," she whispered. Her sparkly pink glossed lips matched her shimmery shirt. My black jeans matched her black heart.

"I hurt my ankle," I explained. I rubbed it for emphasis. I was glad to be out of the roller skates and into my comfy Converse.

Gabi raised her eyebrows and said, "Olivia!"

"Well, I didn't know," Olivia shot back as she twirled her perfectly bobbed blond hair with her index finger.

Brooke and her mom stood up and set aside the black garbage bag filled with wrapping paper. You could totally tell they were mother and daughter. Both were tall and thin with long, stick straight hair the color of chocolate. They both even had a dimple in their right cheek. Brooke's mom looked like she was ready to say something. I pretended to be very interested so I wouldn't have to speak to Olivia.

"We still have time for a party game, girls," Brooke's mom announced. "Everyone loves a manicure, so we are going to do a fun game of Spin the Nail Polish!"

I looked at Gabi to see if she would groan with me, but she beamed. She's such a girl.

All fifteen of us sat around the large, round table. Brooke's mom set eight bottles of nail polish in the middle of the table in a circle with her perfectly manicured hands. She was wearing a French manicure. She then placed a water bottle in the middle of the circle of polish. I scanned the colors. There was candy-apple red, hot pink, royal blue, bright turquoise, silver glitter, a neon green, a melon color, and light pink.

Brooke, of course, spun first. She grinned as she painted her thumb nail turquoise. Next was Olivia. She said, "Ooooh, sparkly!" as she painted her pinky nail silver. We went around the circle. My turn. I spun. Great. Neon green. I grabbed the bottle and painted my left pinky nail the horrid color. Gabi got pink. She giggled and said, "This is fun!"

We continued for about twenty minutes until everyone's nails were complete. My right hand had three blues, a silver, and a hot pink. My left hand had neon green, candy apple red, turquoise, and two hot pinks.

I turned to blow on my nails, and I saw my mom at the front of the rink holding Gerard. She waved to me and walked back outside. Good, I could leave. My ankle had started to throb. I never thought I'd be happy to see that baby. I couldn't wait to go home and take off the hideous nail colors.

"Gotta go," I said to Brooke. "Thanks for the party."

"See ya, Stef!" she called back. The rest of the girls waved or yelled their goodbyes to me.

I turned and walked towards my mom with a slight limp. Then I heard a shriek and an eruption of giggles behind me.

Well, great. The party gets lively when it's my time to leave. I turned around to see what was so freaking funny. Everyone was laughing at me, and I whipped my head forward to see if someone near me had fallen, then back towards the girls and realized, yes, they were laughing at me. Except Gabi. She had one hand over her mouth. She pointed to the back of her pants with the other.

"OMG, Stef! Even your underwear is black!" Olivia yelled.

Well, black with tiny white polka dots to be exact. It's not easy finding black underwear in kids' sizes. I reached back and felt my jeans. I found a tear right down the middle of my butt. I must have torn my jeans when I fell.

Even though my ankle hurt like heck, I tied my coat around my waist and shot out the door. I heard Gabi calling name as I left, but I kept going to the embarrassment-free zone of Mom's car.

I guess my jeans were too tight after all.

Chapter Five

One of the good things about Sundays was sleeping in. I had church at ten with the fam, but at least I didn't have to get up anytime before 9. So I slept until 9 like any twelve-year-old in their right mind would do.

Dad whispered into my room, "Psssst. Stef. Get up for church, hon."

I don't know why he whispered since the whole point was to wake me up.

I grumbled, "I'm up," and rolled out of bed, and I mean I literally rolled out of bed. Of course I landed on my already sore ankle. Ouch. Lyric lifted her head off my pillow and checked on me with her big brown eyes when she heard the thump. She then laid her head back down. Lyric liked to hog the bed and had managed to inch me to the very edge last night. I quickly forgave her and scratched her soft ear before heading down.

I limped down each stair one by one. I heard Dad belting out "Life is Beautiful" in the kitchen. Mom liked to play a song with a positive message each morning. It's one of her *things*. Mom and Dad were already dressed for church. Dad wore a navy button- down with jeans, and Mom wore black leggings with a long, royal blue sweater with a belt slung around her hips. Her dark brown hair was pulled back in a low ponytail. Gerard wore a green sweater vest over a green-and-blue checkered shirt with blue corduroys. Mom loved to dress him up like he was a doll. And today that doll was dressed like an accountant (no offense, Dad).

Dad handed me a glass of orange juice. "Your ankle still hurt, Stef?"

I took the juice and nodded emphatically. I secretly hoped I could stay home and watch TV instead of going with my family to church today.

"Okay, little lady. I'll get some ice for you, and then you'd better eat something before church."

"But my ankle, Dad. Maybe I should stay home," I pleaded with my brown eyed puppy dog look.

"I'll carry you in if I need to," he said. "You are going." He patted me on the head like a dog. I smirked. I could admit that was funny.

I sat at the kitchen table and put the ice on my ankle. It actually wasn't hurting too badly now. I thought it was my ticket out of church, but I guess I was going.

Dad handed me a piece of wheat toast with strawberry jelly. I wolfed it down and went back upstairs to get ready.

Finally, we piled into the family suburban with me and the miniature accountant in the leather bucket seats in the middle row. The bench seat in the last row was always down to fit Dad's band equipment.

Dad remarked, "Hey, why don't we go to that new pancake house for brunch after church?"

"Yes!" I yelled. Gerard jumped and started crying.

"Stef!" Mom turned around and waved a rattle in front of Gerard. It didn't take him long to settle down, like it didn't take her long to snap at me.

"Sorry! I was just excited about us actually going out to a restaurant," I sulked. We hardly ever go anymore, because it's harder with a fussy baby.

Dad tried to keep the peace. "Ladies, all is good now. Who wants to see who can eat the most blueberry pancakes?!"

"Me! But I'm having chocolate chip pancakes with extra whipped cream," I said in a calmer voice than before. I peeked at Gerard to make sure I didn't disturb him again. God forbid.

"I'm out. I still have ten pounds of baby weight to lose," Mom lamented as Dad stopped the car in the church parking lot. She really did have a little more than ten to lose, but I'd never tell her that.

"You look great, babe." Dad smiled and pinched her butt as she got out of the car.

"We're in a church parking lot, dear," Mom said with one eyebrow raised. She lifted Gerard out

19

of the car, and we walked as a happy – okay, *somewhat* happy -- family of four to the church.

I waved to Jenna near the front as we sat down in the second-to-last pew. Mom liked to sit in back in case Gerard fussed. I sat at the end, farthest from the baby. He liked to pull my hair. Who needs that? My eyes glazed over, and I pretended to listen to Father Timothy. Before the offering song, Jenna stood and walked up to the pulpit, her bright yellow dress swishing behind her. She sometimes sang with the chorus. She did have a decent voice. I liked to sing, too, but I wasn't quite ready to have an audience.

Jenna stood in front of the microphone and started singing a solo. Her mom beamed in the front row. Jenna's voice traveled over the pews in a melodic wave. Goosebumps traveled up my arms. I caught myself smiling despite my sour morning mood. Her voice reminded me of Kelly Clarkson's a little bit. As the offering basket came our way, I passed it to my dad so he could place our envelope in. Out of the corner of my eye, I noticed a quick tussle then the loud cry of my baby brother. Gerard's hands grasped the basket full of envelopes and dollar bills, and there was no way the tiny accountant was letting go of the basket of money. My mom faked a thin smile as she tried to pry Gerard's tiny fingers off the basket. He screamed. I looked around. Jenna winced as she continued her song. Row by row, churchgoers looked back at the commotion. Some with angry eyebrows. Some with mouthed O's. Some shaking their heads. Haven't they heard a baby before? Surely Gerard wasn't the first child to interrupt a service. My defensive stance turned to embarrassment. Mom scooted out of the pew with Gerard. Gerard threw a few dollars in the aisle as they rushed out. Jenna's microphone squeaked with feedback as her mouth drew closer to the microphone for more volume. Her head jerked back, and she continued to sing.

Mom took Gerard in the foyer and bounced him up and down. He continued to bawl and bawl. I scooted lower into the pew. Finally, just a few seconds before Jenna's song ended, Mom walked out of the church so he wouldn't disturb the rest of the service. Jenna smiled and patted her dress down as she returned to her pew. Her mom hugged her and whispered into her ear. Well, at least I could sit in peace for the remainder of the hour without a stupid baby grabbing at my hair or drooling on me.

Dad and I filed out as the mass ended. Jenna and her family were getting into their car as we approached the parking lot. "Beautiful job, Jenna!" my dad called to her.

Jenna smiled, "Thanks!" She loved attention.

"You were pretty great, Jenna." I ran over and hugged her hoping she didn't realize it was my brother who ruined her solo.

Backing out of the hug, Jenna pointed to my outfit and cracked, "Yeah, for a second there I thought we were at a funeral with you in black and all the crying."

I cringed. "Sorry about my stupid brother."

Jenna's face relaxed, "I know it's not your fault. But it sure makes me glad to be an only child. See you tomorrow, Stef!"

I waved and hustled to the car relieved that she wasn't mad at me. Thankfully Father Timothy's sermon today was about forgiveness. My dad sat ready and waiting in the driver's seat. Mom was sitting in the passenger seat bouncing a whiny Gerard.

I buckled and said, "Time for pancakes!"

Mom set Gerard back in his car seat and shook her head. "There's no way I'm taking this fussy baby to a restaurant."

"Aww, man!" my dad and I said in unison.

"Maybe just Dad and I could go," I tried.

"Yes, that would be fair," Mom said. "You and Dad enjoy yourselves, and I'll stay home again with a crying baby. Because I really don't do that often enough."

"Okay, then you and me," I tried again.

Mom sighed and said, "I really don't need those extra calories. Let's just go home."

"But!" I started.

Dad turned back at me and gave me a look. "How about I whip something up at home?"

"That would be nice," Mom said.

We rode the rest of the short drive in silence except for a whine here and there from the baby. Gerard had a wonderful way of ruining my day.

Of course we didn't have pancake mix and only one egg. So Dad just made an egg sandwich for himself, and Mom and I had oatmeal. Mom put some frozen blueberries in the oatmeal to try and make up for my missing pancakes. But of course it didn't. Dad promised he'd get some mix so I could have pancakes tomorrow. We'd see if Gerard would ruin that plan, too.

Chapter Six

I strutted into my homeroom on Monday morning wearing my favorite long black boots with my black jean mini-skirt and black tights. My ankle felt strong, and my mom had made my promised blueberry pancakes for breakfast with extra syrup. We had state testing this week, so she made me a bigger breakfast than usual. Plus she probably felt guilty about her crabbiness yesterday. Pancakes always put me in a better mood. Gerard was still sleeping when I left, so I didn't have to deal with him either.

As I passed by Brooke and Olivia, I noticed them whispering to each other. Brooke was wearing the bright, lime green shirt that Olivia gave her at the party. I waved to them. Brooke waved with her multi-colored manicure. I noticed Olivia also still had her nails painted from the party.

"How's your ankle?" Brooke asked.

"Great," I answered. I noticed the girls checking out my scrubbed fingernails.

"Ohhhh," Brooke whined. "I was hoping everyone from my party would have the crazy nails today. It was the talk of the school bus. Anyway, we wanted to talk to you about something."

Olivia squirmed a little, and Brooke nodded to her.

"What?" I asked.

"Hey, Stef," Olivia said. "Brooke and some of the girls were wondering. Why do you always have to wear black? There are so many pretty colors to choose from. It's a little boring, don't you think?"

There went my good mood. My shoulders slumped and I replied, "I like black." I hurried to my desk before she remembered to tease me about my black underwear.

I heard Olivia say loudly, "I mean the invitation did say to wear pink! Hmph!"

Yeah, she meant for me to hear that.

After Mrs. Stark took attendance, she told us to get out our #2 pencils for the state reading test. We took three tests last week. There were three more to go – one today, one tomorrow and one more on Wednesday. I couldn't wait until we got back to our regular school routine. I sharpened my shiny black pencils. The test took almost an hour.

The rest of the day didn't get any better. Olivia knew how to spread gossip faster than Randall Padilla played guitar notes. Randall is the World Record holder for fastest notes played on a guitar per second. 23.5 notes per second! If only I could stuff those notes in Olivia's big mouth.

Olivia must have told everyone about my supposed wardrobe problem, because Kat told me about a new store on Wright Street that carried "fun, colorful clothes." Jenna boldly asked me how many pairs of black underwear I owned while she walked with me to chorus. Skyler asked me if I was a Goth girl.

"What's a Goth girl?" I asked Gabi during social studies.

"Goth girls are girls that wear all black and try to act moody all the time," Gabi told me as she examined her nails. Her nails were still bright and colorful from the party, too.

"I'm usually cheerful!" I screamed a little too loudly. Our social studies teacher, Mrs. Schulte, gave me a stern look. I stared into my textbook, my face burning as I tried to finish my worksheet on the southern states, but it was hard to concentrate.

"Since you have been busy with tests this week, you may finish this tomorrow in class," said Mrs. Schulte. The class cheered.

"Well, at least something good happened today," I mumbled to myself.

I went to my locker and put my black North Face jacket on. I loaded my books into my black and white zebra backpack.

Olivia accidentally bumped into me on the way to her locker.

"Oops! Excuse me, Goth girl," she snickered.

Brooke raised her perfectly arched eyebrow and said, "You really should try wearing different colors, Stef."

"Yeah. It's not like you are a rock star," Olivia continued with her hand firmly on the hip of her tangerine capri pants.

It took everything I had in me to ignore Olivia, but I did. I managed to look Brooke in the eye. "Whatever," I said and waved them away with a flick of my hand. Olivia rolled her eyes, and they took off for their next class. I'm glad they did, because I was afraid they heard my heart pounding against my rib cage. I did not want them to think they were getting to me, but I had to admit they were. I liked black. But I guess wearing something else couldn't be that bad, could it?

"I can't believe you didn't smack her," Gabi said, and then my stomach tensed. This time it wasn't because of Olivia. Josh walked our way past Olivia and Brooke. Or I should say swaggered our way. I could barely see his eyes, because his hair brushed over them. His Megadeth t-shirt looked like it was too big on him. I wondered if it was his older brother's shirt. Man, why does he make me feel so nervous?

Crap! He saw me staring. I felt a bit of sweat form above my lip. Now he probably thought of me as the clumsy girl at the roller rink with a staring problem.

As Josh walked past, I quickly looked inside my backpack. I wasn't looking for anything of course, but I couldn't face him.

Gabi tugged on my arm. "Let's go. What are you looking for in there? Your dignity?"

I smiled in embarrassment. "Well, that's nowhere to be found now."

Chapter Seven

The next morning I started getting dressed as usual. Black jeans, black-and-white striped scoop-necked top. I pulled my medium length brown hair back to show off my sparkly earrings and combed my long bangs just right.

I brushed my teeth while looking into the mirror. Blood pooled in between two of my right-side teeth. I guess I brushed my gums too hard. The bright red actually looked cool against the white of my teeth.

What kind of a freak thinks blood looks cool? I giggled to myself. Then I remembered yesterday. A freak who wears all black.

I tossed my turquoise toothbrush into the holder and looked in the mirror again. Yep. All black. Black jeans, black and white shirt. Even my cuff bracelet was black. But I'm not a freak. I'm just a sixth grader who for the most part gets good grades, plays piano, has slightly weird parents and a pest of a baby brother. But I'm no freak. Is that how people saw me?

Maybe I should wear something different. Just to try it.

"Stefani! The bus is going to be here in five minutes. You need to eat something!" my mom called.

No time to change. I ran down the stairs sniffing the best aroma ever. Mmmm. Bacon. Mom hardly ever made big breakfasts on school mornings, but she always did during state testing. I guess that's one good thing about tests.

My over-easy egg and two slices of bacon waited for me on the table. Gerard wiggled in his high chair eating Cheerios. I sat down next to him and shoveled the bites of egg into my mouth. I picked up my greasy bacon, and Gerard reached for it.

"Bacon is not for babies," I informed him.

He reached for it again, and I waved it in front of his face, "Mmmmmm. Doesn't it smell good? Too bad you can't have any, little brother!" I folded the rest of the bacon in my mouth.

I looked up and saw that Mom was giving me "the look."

I said, "Good bacon, Mom. Thanks! Gotta go!"

"Wash your hands first, Stefani. You don't want grease all over your backpack," my very tidy mother instructed.

I shot a quick spot of foam into my hands and scrubbed up.

"Bye, Mom!"

I started out the door as rain splatted against my face. The bus roared into the neighborhood. I raced back in to put on my shiny, black and silver rain coat and grabbed my backpack before sprinting towards the bus stop.

I ran across my yard towards the corner to the bus stop. I hated being late. Just as the bus slowed to a stop, I felt myself lose balance. Again.

My feet slid on the slick, muddy grass, and I fell to my knees. Right next to the big, yellow bus.

I quickly picked myself up and blinked away my tears. My ankle ached a bit, and I was filthy. They could see me muddy, but they were not going to see my crying. I wiped my face with the back of my hand and boarded the bus amidst giggles.

"It's spring, not fall!" a boy shouted. The bus erupted with laughter and a few whistles. The bus driver looked at me with pity.

I sunk into my seat behind Gabi. More pitiful looks from her.

Gabi tore out some sheets from her purple polka-dotted spiral notebook and handed them to me.

"What are these for?" I asked. "Am I supposed to write a strongly worded letter to Mother Nature?"

"No." Gabi grabbed the papers from me and started wiping mud off my jeans. "They are to get some of the mud off of you! You are a mess!"

I looked down at my jeans. Mud up and down my right leg. Both shoes were covered in mud. Oh, man.

"Thanks a lot!" I said, sarcastically for her comment and genuinely for her help.

We managed to get most of the sloppy mud off, but there was still a big brown stain on my jeans. Good thing I wore black jeans today. Well, not that I would have worn anything else. My black Converse sneakers would need a good washing when I got home. There was mud caked on the black canvas.

"Mud on my socks, mud on my shoes. This brown on my black is giving me the blues. Mud here, mud there, mud everywhere. On my shoes, on my jeans, but not my underwear!" I chanted to Gabi. My dad and I made up silly songs all the time.

Gabi giggled hysterically. "You need to record that little ditty with Quandary!"

"I'll call it, 'Mud Makes Me Mad,'" I snorted. I knew my song would lift my mood.

When we got off the school bus, I didn't even bother trying to cover my clothes from the rain. I was actually hoping it would wash some of the mud off. Gabi ran ahead of me with her pink-and-lime striped messenger bag over her head. Gabi and I were such opposites. I wouldn't be caught dead with a girly pink bag.

Gabi and I became good friends when we were in the same dance class in first grade, and then we ended up having the same teacher in second grade. Can you believe I was in dance? It was fun at first, but I decided not to join again after I had to wear a horrendous polka-dotted yellow dance costume complete with a frou-frou tutu in the dance recital. And I was completely embarrassed when I shuffle ball changed the wrong way and bumped into Larissa Smith during our big dance number to "My Favorite Things." Apparently, I'm not the most graceful person. And apparently, most dance instructors don't pick rock 'n' roll songs for their dance routines. So, I became a dance studio dropout. That's okay, at least I met Gabi because of it. She still takes dance classes, and she's übertalented!

I braced myself for a day with dirty jeans and cruel comments and walked into the school. With a friend like Gabi, I could face anything.

Chapter Eight

I caught up to Gabi in the classroom. The rain didn't help my muddy jeans or shoes at all. In fact, it just made them even more grimy. She sat in the back left corner, so unfortunately we couldn't talk much during class.

At my desk, I traced the carved letters of the initials T.M. with my index finger as everyone in the class sat down around me. I wondered who T.M. was and how in the world did he or she carve it in the desk without Mrs. Stark seeing them. She watched everyone like a hawk.

"Hey, Stef, you took our advice. You aren't wearing all black today!" Olivia slapped me on the shoulder as she walked by.

"What?" I *was* wearing all black.

"I like the brown accents on your jeans," Olivia continued. "They match your eyes." She guffawed like it was the funniest thing she'd ever said in her life. Brooke looked down at my muddy jeans and smiled.

Right. My muddy jeans. I was hoping the brown would blend in more.

"Brown must be the new black," Skyler commented as she sat behind Olivia.

"Very funny," I said. I scrunched my brows in concentration as I finished the last Daily Oral Language problem.

"Ladies, get to work, please," Mrs. Stark warned from her desk.

Thank you, Mrs. Stark. I twisted my cubic zirconia studs in my ears as I looked over my paper. Mrs. Stark reminds us to always check our work before we turn it in. I do sometimes, but now I was really just stalling so I wouldn't have to get up.

I looked at the clock. 9:10. I still had my reading response to do. I needed to turn this in before the bell rang for science.

I brushed my jeans to see if I could get any more mud off of them. They were still damp so it just smeared grime all over my fingers. Yuck.

I quickly turned in my D.O.L. with my clean hand and walked to Mrs. Stark's desk. She was giving Brendan the evil eye for poking Diandra. He saw the look and immediately went back to his paper.

"Mrs. Stark?" I whispered.

"Speak up, Stefani. I can't hear you," she answered while glancing at me over her glasses.

Now I had the class's attention. Super. I could feel all 44 eyes on the back of my black shirt and brown muddy pants leg.

Mrs. Stark noticed, too. "Get back to work, class," she said curtly as she smoothed out her crisp, striped oxford. She looked over her glasses at me, "Yes? What do you need?"

"Um…" I shuffled my feet. "I fell in the mud at the bus stop, and I was wondering if I could call my mom to get new pants."

Mrs. Stark looked down at my jeans. "My word! You certainly did!"

A large shriek erupted from row three, desk four. I couldn't help but turn around to look. Olivia's hand was clasped over her mouth. Several heads were turned toward her.

"Olivia, go take a slip."

Olivia knew the drill. She filled out a behavior slip a few times a week, usually for talking out of turn. She's a chatty one. She even had lunch detention with Mrs. Stark last month for having two slips in one day.

Mrs. Stark handed me the hall pass, and I left as quickly as my muddy Converse could take me. What a relief to leave the watchful eyes of my classmates for a few minutes.

Luckily I checked to make sure my muddy shoes weren't leaving a trail on the floor, because I just about stepped into a pile of vomit on the tile floor. As gross as it was, I couldn't resist inspecting it for a few seconds. I think I saw cereal in there. Yep, there's a few Crunch berries. Ew.

The distinct smell of the red sawdust mixed with puke filled my nostrils. I stepped up my pace to get away from the rancid smell.

As I walked into the office, the school secretary, Mrs. Rodriguez, talked on the phone. She held up one finger to me to tell me to wait a sec. While I waited, I read a poster on the brick wall about a school assembly tomorrow. I was sure it would be lame whatever it is.

"Yes, he's in the nurse's office now....with a bucket. Okay, I'll see you soon. Thank you."

Mrs. Rodriguez must be talking to the puker's mom. She reminded the mom to bring a bucket or bag for the car ride home. I guess I wasn't the unluckiest kid at school today. She hung up the phone.

"Can I help you, Stef?" Mrs. Rodriguez asked with a smile. I don't know how she kept everyone's name straight.

"I fell in the mud on the way to school. Can I call my mom to bring me a new pair of pants?"

"Sure, hon. What's the number?" She dialed my phone number with a pencil as I dictated it and handed me the phone.

The phone rang and rang. The voicemail came on. The usual, "Hello, we love you won't you tell us your name? The Lucases will call you back again," to the tune of a Doors song sang in my ear. That's my family all right. Beep!

"Mom, can you please bring a new pair of pants to school? Mine are wet and muddy. Thanks, bye."

Where is my mom? She is usually at home with the baby…

"May I try again, Mrs. Rodriguez?" I asked.

"Of course," she typed in the number for me. She didn't even have to ask me for it again. That woman was amazing!

Ring. Riiing. Riiiing. Riiiing. "Hello, we love you. Won't you…" I hung up. I hoped she'd bring me jeans when she got the message.

"Not home, huh?" Mrs. Rodriguez said. "Come here. Let me take a look at your pants. You did quite a number on them."

She grabbed some wet wipes from a container on her desk and scrubbed my pants some more. The wipes turned brown, but the jeans looked the same.

"Thanks anyway, Mrs. Rodriguez. I better get to class," I said as I left the office.

I walked briskly to class and dodged the vomit at the last minute.

"UGH!" came out of my mouth as I sidestepped the puke.

Olivia walked around the corner and exclaimed, "Oh, my God, did you hurl?"

"No, Olivia. It looks like it's been there a while," I huffed back.

"But I just heard you!"

I turned and pointed to the vomit. "No, I did not have Cap'n Crunch for breakfast this morning. I had bacon and eggs, thank you. I just almost stepped in it."

Olivia looked at the vomit again and then down at my shoes, and gagged a little. "You *almost* stepped in it? You *did*! Look on your shoe!"

I looked down. Yup, there it was. Mixed with the dried mud, there was the slightest bit of light brownish regurgitate and a bright yellow piece of cereal on the side of my Converse. Not much, but still gross. And it doesn't take much for Olivia to spread gossip around the school.

"Excuse me, ladies," Mr. Z, the custodian, interrupted. Mr. Z was built like an oak tree. He had to be the tallest, sturdiest man I'd ever seen. When I first came to Lakeside, I was scared of him, but I quickly learned he was a big guy with a big heart after he helped me and Brooke look for her lost contact in the hallway last year. He somehow found it stuck to a broken green tile near the lockers. Brooke was so thankful, because she hated wearing glasses. Mr. Z smiled even when he was doing the dirtiest jobs. Like today. He had a mop ready to depukify the hallway.

Olivia gagged again and zipped off to the bathroom clutching the bathroom pass.

"Mr. Z?" I wanted to get his attention before he started.

"Can you?" I pointed to my shoe and then to his mop.

"Sure thing, little lady. Sorry I didn't get here sooner to clean it up." He sprayed something on a paper towel and handed it to me with his huge hands. I guess the mop would have been too sloppy.

I held my breath and scooped the tablespoon of stomach sludge off my shoe with the paper towel and threw it away in the nearest garbage can. I rechecked my shoe. Better. Still muddy, but better. I can't believe I stepped in puke. Disgusting.

I stopped at the bathroom and quickly washed my hands before Olivia came out of the stall. I power-walked to class. I didn't want her to get there first and tell the whole class I stepped in throw-up.

I hung the office pass by the doorway of the class and slunk into my seat. Olivia entered two minutes behind me. Olivia tapped Brooke on the shoulder, but the bell rang.

Everyone gathered up their books. I bolted and walked as fast as I could to science class. Thankfully Olivia wasn't in my science class. Another reason to love science today. I waved to a couple of girls from chorus as I ducked into the science lab.

As soon as everyone was seated, Mr. Millston got right down to business. "Please take out two sharpened #2 pencils. It is time for our next test."

I took a few deep breaths and rummaged through my backpack for my black pencils.

Mr. Millston recited the required spiel before the state test and wrote the start time and end time on the chalk board. "You may begin. Good luck," he said. Twenty heads bent down to start. I whipped through the first five questions, carefully filling in the correct circle. Science was definitely my best subject. This test was probably the best thing that happened all day.

After I finished the test, I silently read while everyone else finished. I concentrated on the four friends in *The Sisterhood of the Traveling Pants*. I guess no one would want to borrow these jeans today, not that Gabi would fit in them. She's five inches shorter than me. The only other girl in my class who was as tall as me was Brooke. I kept my head in my book so I wouldn't think about Olivia spreading rumors about my puke escapade. I decided to just relax and enjoy my book.

Mr. Millston interrupted chapter five, "And stop. Close your test booklet, and place it at the end of your table."

He glanced at the clock. "Class, it's almost time for the bell to ring. I'll call the quietest table to file in line first."

Mr. Millston hated how everyone rushed to the door when the bell rang. He kept his beakers clean and organized and his students orderly.

I stuck my bookmark in and tossed my book into my backpack. I looked over at Jonathan across from me, motioned him to hurry up and sat up as straight as I could. I wanted to get out of here first.

"Table three may line up," Mr. Millston said. My table lined up by the door.

The bell rang and the line pushed behind us. Impatient hormonal preteens. I walked to my locker by Mrs. Stark's classroom. Gabi leaned against my locker with a concerned look on her face.

"Hey, Gabi!" I smiled as I noticed her looking down to inspect my shoes. My smile turned upside down. "Oh, man. You already heard?!"

"About your puke pedicure?" Gabi said. "Sorry, Stef. I think everyone heard."

"That Olivia!" I slammed my locker.

"Don't worry, Stef. Everyone knows she's a gossip girl," Gabi sympathized.

We walked together until Gabi turned down the hallway for art class. She squeezed my arm before she ran off to her class.

My stomach tightened a little as I walked the hall towards the chorus classroom. I usually saw Josh in this hallway as he walked to the gym for P.E. Jenna jogged in her pink sparkly Skechers to catch up with me.

"Stef, Stef, Stef," she murmured as she shook her head.

"Yeah, I know. Gross, huh?" I was preoccupied with scanning the hallway for Josh. Half of me wanted to see him, but the other half didn't in case he'd heard about the puke incident. Not to mention my spill in front of the bus!

42

"Def disgusting," Jenna said. She knocked my backpack askew as she flung up her arm and waved, "Oh, hey, Charlie!"

I adjusted my backpack and looked over to where she'd called. Charlie looked towards Jenna and raised his head in acknowledgement. And walking right next to him was Josh! Josh casually gazed our way but didn't say anything. Which is probably a good thing after the day I had.

Jenna grabbed my arm and squealed in my ear, "Did you see that? Charlie nodded 'Hi' to me!"

"Yes, I saw," I told Jenna. I decided to keep to myself that I noticed he had sweat stains on the armpits of his navy polo shirt.

"Seventh graders are so hot," Jenna sighed. I couldn't disagree with that.

We walked into chorus with goofy smiles that could only be caused by images of cute seventh-grade boys in our minds.

Chapter Nine

P.E. was my last class of the day. I loved that it was last, because I didn't have to worry too much about my slightly wavy hair being frizzy all day. P.E. was okay. I'm a good runner, but I'm not that coordinated so certain team sports like basketball are not my favorite. This week we're learning square-dancing. Yep, square-dancing.

As if corny country music isn't annoying enough, I heard from Jenna that we might have to dance with the boys on the last day of the dance unit. Luckily, for the past few days the girls practiced with the girls, and the boys practiced with the boys. Gabi and I were partners all week. She caught on to routines quickly. She helped me learn better than I would have with another partner. She had serious moves, and she could teach them to klutzes like me.

Yep. The big Dance-Off was today. A huge banner hung over the double gym doors. And if that weren't embarrassing enough, we probably had to dance with the boys today. Boys that were shorter than us and had bad breath. Gabi and her partner would probably win the trophy. She's that good.

The P.E. teachers, Mr. Frawley and Mrs. Hardy, stood in the middle of the gym wearing cowboy hats, and fake leather holsters filled with extra Kleenex and ballpoint pens were slung around their black track pants. Their usual green polo shirt with our eagle logo completed the awful ensemble. They really got into this unit.

I stood between Brooke and Gabi on the black line with the rest of the girls, and the boys lined up opposite the girls on the red line.

"Howdy, pardners!" Mrs. Hardy tipped her hat. "Today we are going to have our square dancing contest. Y'all get in line to receive your dancing partner."

"Do we have the dorkiest gym teachers or what?" Brooke whispered to me.

I smiled and twanged, "Darn tootin!"

She giggled. I was glad the attention was on them and not me for once today.

I gazed at the line of boys dressed in their white t-shirts that read Lakeside with a large green eagle. Some looked smug; some looked horrified. Their shorts were kelly green with two white stripes down the sides. The girls' issued gym uniform was basically the same, except our shirt was green with white writing with the same shorts as the boys. We looked like walking cucumbers.

Mrs. Hardy started counting the girls off one to eighteen and then the boys. I was so nervous, I didn't pay attention to which boy was my partner. It was either the new kid from Wyoming or the know-it-all from science class. That kid got on my nerves because he assumed that because I'm a girl, I didn't know my science. I sure showed him when I scored a 98% on our last science test and he got a 95%. With my luck today, I knew my partner was going to be him though.

"Hope y'all got yer dancin' sneakers on, because it's time for you and your pardners to line up! Cowboys, walk over and introduce yourself to the ladies."

I looked over at Mr. Know-It-All expecting him to come toward me, but he had his hand extended for Gabi to shake.

"Howdy, Gabi. I'm Stef's friend from science, Robert," Mr. Know-It-All said. He thinks he's my *friend*?

Gabi politely shook hands with him and then wiped her hand on her gym shorts when he bent down to tie his shoe. Mr. Know-It-All must also be Mr. Sweaty Hands.

If Mr. Know-It-All was with Gabi then my partner must be…

"Hi, I'm Dakota," a sandy-haired boy said to me. It was the new kid from Wyoming. He looked me straight in the eye. He was the same height as me. I'm taller than most girls, and most of the boys in my grade are shorter than me.

"Hey, I'm Stef." I shook his hand. It wasn't sweaty at all. In fact, he gripped my hand firmly until I unlocked his grasp and put my hand on my hip. I didn't know what else to say, so I looked at Mrs. Hardy to see if she was ready to give directions.

Mrs. Hardy held up two golden square-dance trophies, one in each hand. They were cup trophies about six inches tall with a handle on each side and a circle below the cup with two square dancers in the middle. Mrs. Hardy grinned like she'd just won them herself. Obviously she didn't think they were as tacky-looking as I did.

"These little treasures could be yours if you and your partner work together and do your best. Numbers one to six take your places on the squares. Good luck, y'all. Let the Dance-Off begin!"

Mrs. Hardy placed the trophies on the speakers, and curtsied towards Mr. Frawley. Mr. Frawley removed his hat and bowed, then turned on the country CD. The song was called "Bad Country Song." Not really, but it was a bad country song with the twangs and the fiddlin' and had been stuck in my head for days!

Couples seven to eighteen watched the other twelve square dancers begin their dance. I was so glad I didn't have to dance first. Gabi and Robert were number six. Dakota and I were number seven. Dakota and I stood next to each other while examining our competition. Dakota was tapping his gym shoe to the beat of the God-awful song.

"I've been dancing this dance since I was seven years old," he whispered to me. "My grandma taught square dancing to the kids at the barn dances back home." He grinned real proud.

I bit my tongue so I wouldn't laugh at the poor guy, but I replied, "Cool. Hopefully we won't step on each other's feet then."

I continued to watch Gabi. She was doing really well, but Robert kept messing up. I could see she was getting frustrated. She and I were a pretty good team, especially considering I hated the music. She and Robert looked like they were struggling something fierce.

Thankfully for Gabi, the song ended. All of us on the sidelines clapped for the six couples. Gabi was downright ticked off. She is very proud of being a good dancer, and Robert totally threw them off. She walked to the sidelines with her lips in a tight, straight line and her hands on her hips. Robert pulled up his shorts and walked behind her with a smile.

"We were great!" he told Gabi.

Gabi was much more polite than me, so I knew she was really mad when she huffed, "Seriously?!" at him.

His eyes squinched like a slapped pup. He really didn't know how bad he was. Even Mr. Frawley walked over, patted Robert on the shoulder and said, "Every trail has puddles, son."

And every gym teacher has their weird sayings.

Mrs. Hardy drawled, "All righty, groups seven to twelve, it's your turn to shine!"

Dakota and I stood at our respective spots on the square. Brooke and her partner stood ready and waiting at our square. Olivia and her partner waited at the square next to us.

Olivia called to me, "Stef! Be careful! Don't slip on any vomit while you're dancing!"

Dakota asked, "What's that all about?"

I shook my head and said, "Nothing. Let's do this."

At least Olivia wouldn't be watching me dance. I was so sick of her comments already today.

"Bad Country Music" began.

I held my breath and looked at Dakota. He smiled. We high-tenned each other as we met in the middle of the square. He linked arms with me and turned me for eight counts. I started to stumble at one point, but he grabbed me tighter to brace me. Dakota turned and linked with my right arm for another eight counts. He was right; he knew exactly what he was doing. I barely had to think about the dance with Gabi's instruction all week and his expertise. He led me the whole way.

We do-si-doed and then right-hand starred. Dakota whispered, "Smile!" I realized I was grimacing as I counted the beats.

"Grand left and right," Mrs. Hardy called.

Dakota pulled me by the right hand and passed me. I took Brooke's partner's left hand (Was his name Eli? Ed? Anyway, the short dude with the short name.) and walked back to where we started.

We repeated the whole dance one more time, and the song ended.

Dakota yelled, "Yeah!" He knew he'd nailed it.

Gabi hugged me when I returned to the sidelines with her.

"You two were awesome! What was your partner's name? Austin?" she whispered.

"Dakota. He's one country bumpkin that can dance." I cupped my hand and whispered in her ear so he wouldn't hear me. I didn't want to make him feel bad since he had saved me from one more embarrassing feat today.

We all watched the rest of the couples do their country thing. The girls hung out in a group on the sidelines. The boys hung together to the right of us. Mrs. Hardy and Mr. Frawley wrote comments and critiques in small spiral notebooks as they judged the dancers. They took this way too seriously.

Dakota inched his way next to me halfway through the song.

"Look at these tenderfoots," Dakota scoffed.

I just shrugged my shoulders and replied, "I guess." I thought everyone did pretty well actually. There were some mess-ups here and there. One boy even counted out loud as he danced, but no one fell or tripped or anything like that. Not even me.

When the song ended, Mr. Frawley instructed our groups to do a cool down walk around the gym three times while he and Mrs. Hardy chose the winners.

The P.E. teachers huddled together in the corner of the gym, talking with their brows furrowed. This was serious stuff, you know.

Gabi and I walked together. She had to walk fast to keep up with me. Her shorter legs couldn't keep pace with my long legs. I didn't love being taller than most of the people in my class, but my mom said I will love being tall one day. She said the boys will catch up in high school. I certainly hoped so.

Mr. Frawley blew the whistle, and everyone froze. He blew it again and said, "Take your spots."

We lined up on our spots that were designated in the beginning of the school year. I wondered who was going to win since Gabi was obviously out of the running now with her oaf of a partner.

"Mr. Frawley and I are pleased as punch to announce the winner of this year's Dance-Off! Congratulations to Dakota and Stefani! You are this year's Square Dance Champions!"

My mouth dropped open.

"We won, Stef! I knew we would! You and I were in apple pie order," Dakota picked me up and swung me around. I giggled despite myself. I don't know if I was giggling at the nonsense he just said or the ridiculousness that a rock chick like me just won a square-dance competition. Dakota hooted and hollered like he just won an MTV Video Music Award instead of a dumb P.E. competition.

Dakota took my arm and raced to Mrs. Hardy. The class clapped for us.

"Hold up your trophies while I take your picture for the school newspaper," Mr. Frawley said.

Good God. Our picture in the newspaper?

The camera flashed as I stood next to Dakota. He held his trophy high. I just stood there stunned with my mouth wide open and the trophy held in front of me waist high. I'm sure I looked like a deer in the headlights. I couldn't believe we won.

"Well done, everyone! Now giddy up to the locker room in a line," Mrs. Hardy instructed the class.

Gabi hugged me and yelped, "I can't believe you won! That's awesome!"

Brooke smiled, "Congrats, Stef!"

Olivia mumbled, "Yeah, nice job. I thought you hated country music."

I accepted my accolades with a forced smile and followed the sixth-grade girls into the locker room. The room buzzed with excitement. I was just glad it was over. The competition *and* the day.

We all changed into our regular clothes giggling about the Dance-Off. I started to giggle, too. Finally, the day was about over and I could start a new catastrophe-free day tomorrow. I began to relax. While part of me was mortified that I'd won a country dance competition, I had to admit feeling a little pride over it, too.

I quickly pulled on my muddy black jeans so no one had time to peek at my black undies. As I buttoned my jeans, I noticed that my abdomen was sore. I'd felt knots in my stomach on and off for hours. I shook my head to forget the tumultuous day.

"Who picked these hideous gym uniforms anyway?" I asked no one in particular as I folded my P.E. t-shirt.

"It's not easy being green, is it Stef?" Olivia mocked as she brushed her golden hair. She and Brooke were dressed and ready to go.

Brooke raised her eyebrow and said, "You look good in green, Stef. Why don't you try wearing something colorful to school tomorrow." She cocked her head and said, "In fact, I dare you."

"I double-dare you!" Olivia demanded. "And puke on your shoe doesn't count as another color."

Gabi gasped and looked at them, and then at me. I was so aggravated, I couldn't speak. I just ignored them and poked my head into my gym locker pretending to look for my black bracelet until I heard them leave the locker room.

"Can't wait to see what you wear tomorrow, champion!" Olivia called as she left.

"So? Are you going to take that dare?" Gabi asked when the coast was clear.

53

"I just want to get out of here!" I grumbled as I threw my gym clothes into my gym locker. I stuffed my trophy into my backpack and high-tailed it out of the locker room. This was one big roller coaster of a day, and I just wanted to go home.

Chapter Ten

Gabi and I shuffled out of school and boarded the bus. I tried to keep my eyes from watering as I walked down the aisle, which seemed extra-long today. A seventh-grader whispered, "Goth girl" as I passed. Finally, I plopped into my assigned seat and sighed a little sigh.

Gabi peered around the back of the tall, forest-green seat and asked, "Are you okay, Stef?"

"I'm fi-ine," I sang to her as I picked at the hole in the vinyl seat in front of me. My dad told me that music always made him feel better. It didn't work this time.

"Why do girls even care about my clothes?" I asked. "I like what I like. I wish they'd take a hike!" I almost smiled when I realized I made a rhyme, but I was just too upset.

Gabi pleaded, "Why don't you wear yellow or purple tomorrow? Even red! Just to stop them from teasing you."

I sang to her, "I will wear what I wear. I don't care if they care." I smiled, because I meant to make that rhyme. It was like a lyric from a song. Like the lyrics that Dad wrote for his band. Singing did make me feel a little better this time.

"Well, at least you won today," Gabi tried.

"Me? A square-dance champion? That's not exactly something I'm going to shout from the roof tops." My attitude had definitely soured because of that stupid dare.

The bus stopped. I nodded goodbye to Gabi.

Gabi waved and whispered, "Yellow!" I pretended not to hear as I exited the noisy bus.

I walked to my house and threw my backpack on the couch. I flopped down and closed my eyes.

My mom came in holding Gerard.

"Hey, babe. How was your day?" she asked.

I grunted. Gerard grunted. Then Mom smelled Gerard's behind.

She wrinkled her nose and said, "That bad, huh? Let me change this li'l guy's diaper, and then I'll sit with you."

"Whatever," I grumbled.

Lyric put her paws up on my knees and licked my right cheek. I held her head and put my face into her soft black fur. I sat and hugged her head as she nuzzled me. Dogs love you no matter what you wear.

Lyric was a black Lab mix that we adopted from an animal shelter when I was six. She was the best dog ever.

My mom returned a few minutes later with a fresh baby. She put Gerard on a blanket on the floor. Lyric hurried over to lick Gerard's face. Gerard squealed and waved his arms at our dog.

"No, no, Lyric. Let's go outside!" My mom let Lyric out in our fenced-in backyard and returned to the couch.

"You want to talk about it?" she asked as she put her arm around me.

"No," I answered.

"I'll just let Gerard play with his blocks and sit with you here then," Mom said gently. She snuggled into the soft navy leather couch next to me. I put my head on Mom's shoulder.

"Did you see my jeans?" I asked.

"Goodness! What the heck happened to you?" my mom asked.

"Well, I started off the day falling on my face in front of the whole bus. Then I had to sit with muddy jeans all day at school."

"Why didn't you call me?" Mom said. "I would have brought you some new ones."

"I tried," I accused. "No one answered the phone!"

"Hmmmm. The phone did ring while I was nursing Gerard this morning. I guess I forgot to check the messages," Mom said. "I'm so sorry, Stef."

She did look sorry. And she should be. She put both arms around me.

After a few minutes, I whispered, "Girls are making fun of the way I dress. Because I wear black all the time." I let some tears escape and hid my face in her shirt. I couldn't help it.

My mom hugged me and said, "Oh, honey. I think you always look very cool. You are a beautiful girl. You would look beautiful if you wore all black, all brown, or all purple!"

"You have to say that," I sniffled. "You're my mom."

"I'd say that even if I wasn't your mom," my mom replied. "You wear what you feel most comfortable in. It's nobody else's business. Your friends should like you for you, not for what you wear."

"Some of the girls are teasing me," I whimpered.

"Well, that's no fun. Stef, things will die down. They'll get tired of teasing you after a while. Only you can decide if you want to change how you dress. Don't let them decide for you," Mom said.

"I know," I said. I let Mom hold me for a while longer.

Gerard threw a wooden alphabet block at us. The letter A for annoying.

"I guess someone else wants some attention now," Mom cooed to Gerard.

Of course he does.

Gerard smiled at me. I ignored him. Sometimes I wished he was never born. This was one of those times. I needed my mom, and Gerard stole her away again.

"I better go change and work on my reading homework," I said to my mom. Science was my best subject, but reading was a close second. I did not want to ruin my A in it, even if I was bummed. I only had a few more questions anyway. I should have finished them at school, but I was so distracted by everyone's teasing, I couldn't focus.

I opened up my backpack to grab my notebook.

"What is that, Stef?" my mom asked as she eyed the trophy peeking out of my backpack. She snapped it up.

"Hey!" I said and snatched it back.

Mom turned it in my hand and looked at the square dancers on the trophy. She covered her mouth. I think she was trying not to laugh.

"Did you win this?" Mom asked with a smirk.

"Yeah, as if my day wasn't embarrassing enough," I said.

"Wow! This is awesome, Stef. I'm proud of you," she patted my shoulder. "You can't just go upstairs and not tell me more about this. Spill it!"

I sighed and gave her the shortest version of the Dance-Off that I could muster, "It was a dance contest in gym class. My partner was some new guy from Wyoming who loves square dancing, and we won. That's it. No big deal."

"Well, it is a big deal," she said to me. She looked at Gerard and said, "Who knew your sister could square dance?"

I tilted my head and rolled my eyes.

As I started up to my room, my mom called to me, "I almost forgot! Tomorrow Dad has a special surprise for you! I know you'll have a better day, honey."

"Thanks, Mom," I said. Tomorrow had to be better.

Chapter Eleven

The next morning I surveyed the wardrobe hanging in my closet. Black pants, black skirts, black dresses, black blouses, black t-shirts, and a black leather jacket stared back at me. In the back corner, I could see a lavender-colored shirt peeking from behind my poufy black tulle skirt. There was also a red and white long sleeve top that I got for Christmas from Grandma Jo and a turquoise dress from my cousin Emily.

I tugged on my black leggings and pulled the long lavender top over my head. I looked in the mirror. Weird. I took it off. I sighed and put it back on again.

"It's not that bad," I thought. I added a black vest with silver sequins on it. "That's better," I said to the mirror.

I dug around my box of barrettes and found two purple ones shaped like stars. I brushed my hair and carefully placed the barrettes on each side of my head. I found a purple bangle and slid it on my wrist. I actually had a lot of colorful accessories from various birthdays. I just rarely wore them. Now I was ready as I'd ever be.

I walked down the stairs slowly and carefully. I was in no rush to go to school today. My dad fed Gerard in the sunny kitchen with the TV blaring the news in the family room. Gerard wore his light blue "Mama's Boy" bib that was already stained with something light-colored.

"Mornin', Stef!" he called. "Do you want to help me feed the baby?"

"Nah," I muttered.

"C'mere, honey," my dad persisted. He pulled me in to give me a hug. "Congratulations on your dance contest."

"Thanks, now enough about it already."

He smirked and held out the baby food towards me.

I made a face and said, "Fine. Give me the spoon."

Gerard giggled when I tried to feed him. His life was so easy.

"Here come the bananas," I sang to him. He ate a few spoonfuls and then grabbed the spoon.

"No, baby!" I yelled, but it was too late.

Gerard whipped the spoon at me and squealed with delight.

Banana baby food splattered all over the front of my lavender shirt.

"Thanks a lot, Gerard!" I yelled and ran up the stairs. I knew this was going to be a bad day.

I stomped into my room and sat on the bed. What was I going to wear now? Maybe this was a sign that I should just wear black like I always did. I plopped down on my zebra-striped comforter and stared at the ceiling. What now?

Lyric jumped up on my bed and started licking my shirt.

"Lyric! Get off of me!" I scowled. Not even my dog could cheer me up today.

Lyric scrambled off the bed and trotted downstairs. She's a smart dog.

My mom walked into my room and sat next to me.

"What happened, Stef?"

"Look at what Gerard did to my shirt!" I complained.

"What a mess," she said.

"You think?" I grouched.

My mom ignored my sass and said, "I see you chose to go with some color today. It looks nice." She focused on the stain, "Well, except for the banana all over it," she teased.

"That's not funny. I don't know what to wear now," I said.

"Do you want to wear something colorful today?" she asked.

"I don't have anything else colorful," I said.

"I do have a few shirts I picked up for Emily in my closet. Do you want to try one? I can always get her something else for her birthday," Mom said.

"Fine. Let me check them out," I said.

My mom came in with two shirts on hangers: a short-sleeve yellow polo shirt and a yellow, blue, red and orange tie-dye shirt with a peace sign on it.

"You can still go with all black, Stef. Don't let anyone make you do something you aren't comfortable with," she said.

I thought about what she said for a moment.

"Mom. I'm going to just do it. Give me the tie-dye shirt. Why not? I might as well go all out." I faked a smile.

My mom smiled a real smile and said, "You do what you gotta do, girl."

I took off my banana-stained top and put on the colorful one. I removed the purple barrettes. Mom pulled my hair up and put it in a ponytail with a red bow.

I looked in the mirror and sighed, "Well, here goes nothing."

"Knock 'em dead, kid," Mom said.

We walked down the stairs together.

My dad eyed my mom suspiciously, and she said, "Crisis averted."

"I have your breakfast on the table, Stef," Dad said. He was holding Gerard.

I gave a mean look to Gerard then kissed him since my parents were watching. I guess he can't help being naughty sometimes.

"That's my girl," my dad smiled.

"Why aren't you dressed for work yet, Dad?" I asked.

"I have a special gig today," he answered with an impish grin.

"Oookay," I said, half-listening. I finished my bagel and grabbed my backpack. My dad can be so weird.

It was time for the bus. The confidence I had a few minutes before vanished.

Chapter Twelve

Gabi was waiting for me on the bus. She immediately noticed my red bow.

"Your hair looks cute," she said. She was such a good friend.

I unzipped my black coat to show her my tie-dye shirt.

"Wow! You did it! You look awesome." Gabi's eyes widened.

"Thank you," I said sincerely. "I can't wait to hear what Brooke and the rest of the girls have to say. Or not."

Gabi shrugged and said, "Don't worry about it, Stef."

"Easy for you to say."

"Don't worry about it, Stef," she repeated. "It is easy to say."

"Is everyone a comedian today?" I asked.

I hummed to the music on the bus radio to keep my mind off school.

The bus made every green light and every person was ready at their stop, so of course we were at school in record time.

"Let's go." Gabi grabbed my arm and walked with me into the school. Thank goodness I had her as a friend.

I nervously hung my black jacket in my locker. I felt like the colors from my shirt were blazing through the hallway like a laser show. It didn't take long for someone to notice.

"Well, well, well," Jenna said as she walked by.

I hurried to the classroom. Brooke eyed me up and down and smacked Olivia in the stomach to get her attention.

But it was my stomach that hurt.

Olivia walked up and said, "Hey. I can't believe the Rock 'n' Roll Princess wore something colorful today."

Brooke raised one eyebrow and said, "It looks cute, Stef. Really."

"Ummm. Thanks," I murmured and opened a book. I pretended to read so I didn't have to talk to anyone.

Luckily we had a busy morning with the last state test and two science experiments. I tried not to meet anyone's eyes during class to avoid any conversations. I certainly did not want to be teased yet again.

Chorus was right before lunch. It was my favorite class. It was too bad we only had it for two quarters a year. We had art the other two quarters. Usually we sang short, silly songs meant just for children, but once in a while our music teacher, Miss Lee, would teach us a song by the Beatles or from a Disney movie. Today the lyrics to "Rainbow

Connection" were on our seats when we arrived. Well, that left me wide open for class jokes.

Skyler looked at the sheet and remarked, "Maybe Stef can sing solo today since she's dressed like a rainbow." The class snickered. My face burned, probably a colorful red.

Miss Lee said, "I think all you girls are dressed in beautiful colors today. Let's try just the girls, then just the boys." She started playing the piano.

As I sang with the girls, the heat slowly left my cheeks. Music did usually make me feel better.

I closed my eyes and wondered to myself, "Why are there so many gosh darn songs about rainbows?"

Chapter Thirteen

I was glad to be back in class after lunch since it felt like everyone was staring at me in the cafeteria. Jenna had asked me if I was a groovy girl now instead of a Goth girl. How pleasant. Olivia hummed "Rainbow Connection" when she waited in the hot lunch line behind me. At least my jacket covered up my blazing shirt at recess.

Mrs. Schulte rang her bell to get our attention. "Please read chapter six in your social studies book, and then do questions one to five at the end. Complete sentences please." I bent my head down to get to work. All I could hear was the sound of papers rustling and the scratching of pen on paper. No irritating voices at last.

Mrs. Schulte interrupted my train of thought and announced that we were to line up for a school assembly. I had forgotten about that. With my luck, it was probably a health assembly about the stomach flu, or a fashion show.

Our class walked to the gym and sat down in front of the stage. A drum set, two guitars, and a microphone were set up on stage. Cool. Some sort of concert.

"Stef, maybe we're having a hoedown and you and Cowboy can dance for everyone," Olivia said to me from the back of the line. Someone else yelled, "Yee haw!"

"Oh, that's right," I called back to Olivia. "You lost yesterday." I turned and looked carefully at the instruments. Thankfully the drum set looked more rock than country with the skull on it. The electric guitar almost looked like one of the three that my dad owned.

Gabi whispered as we sat down, "Ha! You told her! The day is almost over, you can relax now."

"I'll relax once I'm at home," I answered. "I'm sure I'll be teased on the bus or at the lockers."

The gym lights dimmed a little, and Principal Hayes tapped the microphone.

"Testing..." she cleared her throat. "Hello, Lakeside Eagles! We have a special performance today that I know you will enjoy. You've all worked so diligently these past two weeks with state testing. Congratulations on all of your hard work. Clap your hands and give a warm welcome to Quandary!"

My mouth dropped open, and I looked at Gabi.

"Awesome!" she squealed. "I've always wanted to hear your dad's band play."

I couldn't believe my dad didn't tell me he was coming today! I clapped my hands.

My dad, my cousin Gina, and Jack, the drummer, all waved to the crowd as they walked onstage. Gina looked beautiful as always with her long dark hair and black high heels. She wore a plain black tank top with a studded belt over her black jeans. My dad had his vintage light-blue Eagles concert shirt on and jeans. I could see his cross tattoo peeking out of his right sleeve. Thankfully Jack had a shirt on today. He usually played without one. He said it gets hot banging on the drums.

I watched my dad scan the audience to look for me. Gabi sat up on her knees and pointed down at my head. I waved a small wave so I wouldn't draw too much attention to myself. He shouted, "Hey, Stef!" He grinned a ridiculous Joker-sized smile.

Everyone in my grade turned their heads toward me. So much for being discreet. Thanks, Gabi.

Gina took the microphone and said, "Hello, Tigers! We're Quandary, and we are so excited to join you today. You all rocked your tests, so now let's rock and roll. We're going to start with an old Runaways song that I changed the words to. Clap along!"

Gina winked at me and said, "Hit it, Stef's dad."

My dad startled the crowd with a cool guitar riff, and Gina started singing. All eyes were glued on her as she sang a junior high rated version of "School Days."

I clapped along, having so much fun. I still couldn't believe my dad didn't tell me he was playing at the school today! My eyes scanned the crowd. Everyone was clapping or moving their heads to the beat. I felt better than I had all day.

"I know you all know this one. Stand up, and sing it with me!" Gina yelled. She started singing the school fight song. Everyone jumped up and sang along. As she began the second verse, she stared at something at the front row with a funny look on her face.

What was she looking at? Everyone else continued to sing.

Gina gasped and dropped the microphone onto the stage with a thump. She leaped off the front of the stage.

What in the world was she doing? I'd never seen Gina stage-dive before.

My dad stopped playing. Everyone stopped singing and then started talking at once. I craned my neck to see what the heck was going on in the front row. Gina had her arms around a boy with shaggy hair. She thrust her fist into his stomach and something pink flew out of his mouth. OMG. The boy was Josh!

Principal Hayes and Josh's teacher, Mr. Danville, crowded around Josh. Mr. Danville then led a shaky Josh to a chair. Josh looked like he might cry. He gave Gina a weak smile as Mr. Danville led him out the gym doors.

Principal Hayes and Gina climbed back up onto the stage. They whispered to each other for a minute. A wide-eyed Principal Hayes spoke into the microphone. "I just wanted to thank our guest, Gina. She saw that a student was choking in the audience and gave him the Heimlich maneuver. Please let's give her a hand."

The crowd roared and clapped.

Gina smiled her wide, red-painted smile as she took the microphone. The event didn't shake her up at all. She was beyond cool. "Your principal would like me to remind you that food is not allowed in the gym. Let's try this again, shall we?" She looked back at Jack who yelled, "1, 2, 3, 4!"

The band played five more songs -- one from the old program "Schoolhouse Rock," "Sing" by My Chemical Romance, two songs that they wrote, and one from the latest Disney movie. Students sang along to the Disney song, and goose bumps formed on my arms! It was so cool to have everyone singing along to my dad's band.

Then Gina kneeled on the stage and said, "We have one more song for you that I want you to think about after school today. Don't forget to treat others the way you want to be treated. Everyone is different. Just be yourself."

Jack hit the drumsticks together, and Gina began my favorite Quandary song called "Be Yourself." I love listening to Gina sing. I mouthed the words along with Gina. Before I knew it, the song ended, and Gina yelled, "Thanks for having us! Have a great day! You rock, Eagles!"

The students and teachers applauded for Quandary. Gabi grabbed my arm and yelled, "Wow!"

That was exactly what I was thinking.

Chapter Fourteen

As we lined up to go back to our room, everyone chatted incessantly about the concert. Javier, who hardly ever spoke in class, gave me a thumbs up and whispered, "So, you know Gina?"

"She's my cousin," I replied proudly.

"You do kind of look like her," said Jenna.

Bonnie, our school's eighth grade hockey superstar, stopped me in the hall. She said, "Wow, Stef! Gina is so brave."

I didn't even know she knew my name. And she was an eighth grader!

All afternoon students smiled at me or gave me a thumbs-up. As the class passed the office, Josh walked out, and he looked his normal self again. He stopped mid-step and caught my eye. At first I was embarrassed that he saw me looking at him, but he gave me the rock 'n' roll devil horns sign and strutted the other way. I giggled out of nervousness and surprise. It looked like he wasn't too traumatized over the whole ordeal in the gym. I sighed out of relief that he was okay.

Gabi grabbed my arm and whispered, "He just…" Then I realized that he had actually acknowledged me for the very first time. He finally noticed me!

I gasped, "OMG!" back to her and felt a surge of happiness that I hoped would never end.

The final bell rang, and I couldn't believe school was over already. I had actually enjoyed myself after the last few days of dreading school. I couldn't stop smiling because of Josh and the concert.

By my locker, I packed up my things then lined up behind Mrs. Stark to go to the buses. Even she remarked, "You have a lot of talent in your family."

"Thanks," I smiled.

Skyler nudged me and said, "I didn't know your dad was a rock star!"

I raised my eyebrows and said, "He isn't. He's an accountant."

We passed by Dakota's locker on the way to the buses. His trophy sat on the top shelf of his locker. He was rubbing it with a red handkerchief. Was he shining it?

"Hey, Dakota!" I shouted. I resisted the urge to use a country accent.

He stuffed his handkerchief in his pocket and waved to us, "Hello, gals!"

Gabi turned to me and beamed, and we hurried to the buses with grins the size of Wyoming.

Gabi and I sang "Be Yourself" quietly on the bus ride home. She knew the words, because we listened to Quandary's demo CD sometimes when she was over to hang out. A few students even chimed in on the chorus with us.

The bus stopped at my corner. My mom was in the garage putting Gerard in his car seat. She waved. I waved back as I stepped off the bus.

"Mom!" I yelled. "Did you know Dad was going to be at school today?"

She laughed. "Of course I did, silly!" She hugged me. "I take it your day was better today?" she smiled.

"It was awesome!" I shouted. I looked at Gerard in his car seat. "Your dad and cousin Gina rocked the school," I told him. He drooled.

"Where are you going, Mom?" I asked.

"I have to run to Target to get a few things," she said as she slid into the front seat. "Hop in and tell me about your day." I threw my backpack on the back seat, scooted in, and buckled.

"My day was unfreakingbelievable!" I blurted. "Gina saved someone's life during the concert!"

My mom stopped backing out of the driveway with a screech and looked back at me. "What?" she shrieked.

"This guy Josh was choking during a song, and she dove off the stage and saved him," I said. "It was unbelievable!"

My mom replied, "That certainly is."

I babbled to Mom about the concert in detail.

My mom said, "I wish I could have been there. It was during Gerard's naptime, and he was up in the night with his teething, so I let him sleep."

Of course Gerard took priority. But I didn't say anything. Mom looked exhausted. "How long will we be at the store? I have a few social studies questions to finish for homework," I said.

"We won't be long," she answered. "I need to get back myself so I can squeeze in some phone calls for the fundraiser. With Gerard, I can never get any of my work at the foundation done anymore."

Mom never complained about Gerard. What was up with that?

Chapter Fifteen

We grabbed a shopping cart at Target and walked through the aisles. My mom put diapers into the cart. We continued to walk through the baby department.

"This is cute," Mom said, holding up a shirt to Gerard. "Anything would look cute on you!" she cooed as she tickled him. Mom put the shirt and a pair of camouflage pants for Gerard in the cart. She must have felt guilty for complaining about the infant prince.

"Let's see. What else do we need?" she murmured to herself.

"Can we get some chocolate milk, Mom?" I asked imploringly. I loved chocolate milk. I'd have it ten times a day if I could, but Mom only let me have it a few times a month. She said that regular skim milk is much healthier. Which it is of course, but it just doesn't have that chocolatey, creamy goodness.

"I guess so. Grab some pomegranate juice, too, please. I'm glad you are in a better mood today, Stef," Mom said.

I quickly placed the chocolate milk and juice into the cart before she changed her mind. Although she was probably too tired to care about my chocolate milk intake. We walked over to the clothes section. Mom put a plain white v-neck t-shirt into the cart. She loves to wear them under the gazillion hooded sweatshirts she has. I looked at the girls' section.

I grabbed a pair of hot pink jeans and said, "Mom! What do you think of these?"

"I think they're cute," she said. "Like you'll ever wear pink."

"Can I get them?" I asked.

"Seriously?" she asked.

"Yep. I am as serious as a Smashing Pumpkins song."

"You have plenty of clothes," Mom said.

"So Gerard gets something, and I don't," I pouted.

"Seriously?" she said again. "I just don't want to buy them and have them sit in your closet."

"Yes, Mom. Black is still my favorite color. But really, why shouldn't I mix it up a bit? I want to try wearing black with a little splash of color here and there. And Gabi always looks good in pink." I felt daring, like anything was possible now.

A look of realization hit Mom's face. "How did your day go with the new shirt?"

I was wondering when she was going to care enough to inquire.

"Those girls didn't change your mind, did they?" my mom asked.

80

"No. I got teased today for wearing tie-dye, and I got teased for wearing black. It really doesn't matter what I wear. And really I do like other colors. I'll still mostly wear black. I mean, come on, that's just me," I explained. "But I think I want to wear other stuff, too. I'm getting older, and I want more choices."

"Sounds good to me," Mom said as she felt Gerard's cheeks. "Hmmm, he feels warm to me." She kissed his forehead.

Mom paced as she paid for our things.

"Gerard must be getting sick," Mom worried. "Maybe that's why he was so fussy all night. Maybe it's just the teething..."

Gerard was a little whiny on the way home, which made Mom fret even more. She barely talked the entire car ride.

Dad was walking Lyric in the front yard when we arrived.

"Hey, girlie!" he grinned. I ran to him and jumped into his arms.

"I can't believe you didn't tell me!" I playfully scolded him.

"So, did the kids love it or what?" he said as he put me down.

"You guys were a hit!" I squealed. "Everyone was talking about it the rest of the day." I paused.

"Can you believe what happened during the concert?" I asked.

"I was wondering what the heck Gina was doing jumping off the stage!" he exclaimed. "Well, it's a good thing she did."

"Yeah, poor Josh," I said. "But he's okay. And so are you." I poked him in the arm.

"Wow," Dad said. "Hey, since I'm Superdad today, I even ordered pizza for dinner. It'll be here in twenty minutes."

"But I was going to make a…," my mom started.

"It's done! I ordered extra anchovies for you," Dad said as he slapped her on the butt.

My mom made a face, but knew my dad was teasing her.

"Hey, watch it," Mom said. "I have to bring Gerard in. He might be coming down with something."

Dad kissed Gerard. "He feels okay to me."

"Da Da! Da Da!" Gerard yelled.

"Everybody loves me today," my dad sang.

"You are a goofball, Dad." I turned to my mom. "I'll bet it's just teething, Mom."

"You are probably right, but I had better nurse him and then take his temperature to be sure." Mom hurried into the house with the baby.

Chapter Sixteen

The next morning I brushed my teeth while I hummed "Be Yourself." I put on my new pink pants and a long-sleeved black t-shirt. I brushed my hair, and I even put on the hot pink headband I wore to Brooke's party. The outfit looked cute, if I did say so myself. I took out some clear lip gloss and dabbed it on my lips. I had full lips and usually tried *not* to draw attention to them. Mom says some people actually inject their lips to look like that. Yikes. I just felt like shiny lips today, and I thought it might be a distraction from my pink pants.

I came downstairs as my dad rushed towards the door to the garage. He was in his usual khaki pants and a button-down shirt.

"Gotta go, honey. Have a great day at school," he said.

"No breakfast?" I asked.

"I can't be Superdad every day," he said. He blew a kiss to us and was out the door.

Mom looked at the clock. "He's late to work. He stayed up late writing songs last night. I think the gig at school inspired him a little."

She looked tired.

"When does Quandary play next? Can I go?" I asked.

"They play at the end of the month at the restaurant by Target. No kid tunes that night, and it starts at nine. Sorry, hon. You'll have to see them another time. They do practice here on Friday, though."

"Sweet! Can I ask Gabi to sleep over then?" I asked excitedly.

"Sure, but we have to get her home by ten on Saturday morning. You have piano lessons. Let's make sure that Gerard feels better, too. He had a fever much of the night."

"Okay," I said. I hoped my brother wouldn't ruin my sleepover.

I finished my cereal bar and ran out to the bus stop.

Gabi waved as I climbed on the bus. I waved my fingers at her as I scanned the back of the bus to see if anyone noticed my flashy pants. Everyone was talking to someone else or reading a book. A few were getting in a last minute snooze. I plopped in my assigned seat behind Gabi.

"Cute pants!" she exclaimed. "I can't believe *you* are wearing *pink*!"

"I know," I said. "Olivia or Skyler will probably torment me today. But who cares."

The bus arrived at our school, and Gabi and I walked to our lockers. I could not believe what I saw.

Jenna shut her locker and said, "Hey, Stef. Hey, Gabi." She was wearing a short-sleeved button down black shirt and a long, black skirt with a slim yellow belt that cinched her waist.

Then Brooke grabbed my arm. "Stef! Your cousin is so cool. Maybe I'll be a singer like her one day."

She glanced down. "Oh! I love your pants!" She walked away.

Gabi said, "Did you see what she was wearing?!"

Brooke was wearing a black tank top, black jeans and a black belt. Almost like Gina's outfit yesterday!

"Whoa," I raised my eyebrows.

Brooke walked to Olivia's locker. Olivia was wearing a gray top with a skull on it with a black mini-skirt. I saw Brooke give her the thumbs up. What was going on?!

So many girls in the hallway had either a black top or black pants on today – sixth graders, seventh graders, even eighth graders. Skyler wore black leggings with a long black sweatshirt. Some of the guys had rock and roll band t-shirts on today, too. Well, Josh usually wore a rock t-shirt most days, but not anyone else. I counted ten boys with rock shirts on today! Well, one had a Katy Perry shirt on and I wasn't sure that even counted. So nine.

My mind was spinning. This was too weird. Did everyone go shopping last night?

At lunch time, I realized I hadn't been teased once today. I thought I'd get some sort of sassy remark about my hot pink pants. Nothing!

Olivia and Brooke walked toward me. Olivia was wearing small black heels with her rock outfit. I could tell she wasn't used to walking in them. She walked very deliberately and slowly.

Brooke asked, "So, when does your dad's band play again? They were awesome!"

Olivia nodded as she teetered on her heels.

"At the end of the month," I said. "Most of their shows are late and for adults though."

"Cool," Olivia said.

"Too bad," said Brooke. "Talk to you later. Jenna wants us." Brooke and Olivia started to walk away when Olivia stopped and eyed my pants and said, "Stef, why didn't you just wear those pants to Brooke's party?"

I opened my mouth to answer, but Brooke pulled Olivia's arm and resumed walking. It looked like she was scolding her.

Then Olivia stumbled and fell on the blacktop. Heels are so not for sixth graders.

Gabi and I looked at each other and giggled. I mean, c'mon. She kind of did deserve that.

"Hey!" I said. "Quandary is practicing in our basement tomorrow night. Do you want to sleep over?"

"Of course," Gabi said. "I'll ask my mom."

"I hope she says yes," I said as the bell rang to go back inside.

When I got home from school, my mom was reading a board book to Gerard on the couch.

"Hey, Pinky!" she smiled. "How was your day?"

"Well," I said. "You are the very first person to tease me today. What do you think of that?!" I didn't wait for my mom to answer.

"And you will NOT believe what the girls wore to school today. BLACK! Yes, black! Black pants, black shirts, black skirts. Olivia even wore black heels!" I exclaimed. Then I smiled to myself thinking about her tripping over her own two feet.

"Well, that is unexpected," my mom said. Gerard tugged at the book.

"Just a sec, baby," she sang to him.

I went on, "I thought Gina told everyone to Be Yourself! They all want to be like Gina!"

"Oooooh, I see," Mom said and nodded. "Gina is gorgeous. She certainly wowed them yesterday in more ways than one."

"It was such a crazy day, Mom. Someone even asked me if Dad was a rock star!" I said.

Mom covered her mouth as she laughed. Gerard even giggled.

I walked over to sit by them and heard a "Crack!" I looked down. Gerard's favorite rattle with the bunnies on it sat smashed in pieces on the floor.

"Oh, no!" Mom exclaimed.

"Oops," I said. I ran to get a bag for the pieces. As I threw the pieces away, Gerard started crying.

"Oh, honey. I wish you'd watch where you're going," she said to me. "That was the only toy that could calm Gerard down today."

It always came back to Gerard. Here I had a great day, and Gerard ruined it. Again. Tears sprang to my eyes.

"It was an accident!" I yelled. "All you care about is that baby!" I ran up to my room.

Chapter Seventeen

I closed my door and threw myself on my bed. I was so sick of my mom always choosing Gerard over me. My mom and I used to do everything together. She'd take me to the movies once a month. Now she couldn't because Gerard was too young to go. We used to play Go Fish and Monopoly on the weekends, but now she doesn't have time. She hasn't even played her turn in Words With Friends in weeks. It's a miracle she has time to make me dinner or take me to piano.

I turned on my iPod stereo. Evanescence should fit my mood. I turned it up enough to drown my thoughts, but soft enough not to get a talking-to. I stretched on my half-made bed with my hands behind my head and stared at the small spider scurrying to the web floating in the corner. Hmmph. Mom didn't even have time to keep my bedroom arachnid-free anymore. I couldn't believe she didn't notice my bed wasn't made either. I heard a knock on the door, and the door opened. My mom came in and sat on my bed. I turned my head so she couldn't see my face.

"Stefani. Please look at me," Mom said. She grasped my hand.

"Stef. I'm sorry I reprimanded you about the rattle. I know it was an accident. I've just been so tired with Gerard being up in the night. That was the only toy that has helped, and I was just disappointed that I couldn't use it anymore for a few moments of reprieve."

Mom turned my face so I'd look at her. "Stef, please talk to me. You can't keep this in."

"You love Gerard more than you love me." I finally said it. I finally said what I feared all along.

"Oh, Stef." My mom cupped my hand with both of hers. "I am so sorry I've made you feel that way. I love you so much. You are my firstborn, my little buddy for the last twelve years."

"Not anymore," I grumbled.

She sighed. "You are right. We don't spend any time just the two of us anymore. I have been so busy with Gerard. It's been so long since I had a baby, it seems overwhelming at times. I had to cut down my hours at the foundation. I had to quit my Pilates class. I'm sorry I didn't realize I was cutting time with you, too."

I never thought that she was missing her old life at all. I just thought she was so wrapped up in the baby, and that was all that mattered. But I didn't say anything.

My mom kept talking. "I'm sorry I didn't realize that you felt left out. When he was first born, you were so helpful. Holding him and bringing me his diapers. Time just flew with your activities,

90

Dad's concerts, and having a baby again. I had no idea you were feeling like this until now."

"Well. I do," I squeaked and a tear escaped and rolled down my face.

Mom hugged me. "How about this. Let's you and I make one day a month a girls day and do something special. We could just go for ice cream. Go shopping. Go to the movies. What do you think? I miss our girl time, too, Stef. I really…"

She stopped mid-sentence to listen for something.

Gerard fussed in the next room. Mom got up to check on him, then turned to look at me. I raised an eyebrow.

"Stef. The boy is sick," she pleaded and left.

And I'm abandoned yet again for my baby brother.

"Oh, no," my mom said from the next room. "He's burning up."

What an emergency! He's got a fever. Big freaking deal.

Beep. Beep. Beep. I heard the thermometer as Mom took Gerard's temperature.

"It's almost 105!" she exclaimed. I walked into Gerard's room to see if he looked that sick.

She grabbed Gerard and pushed me aside as she exited the doorway.

"I have to call Dr. Browne. Stef, will you get your dad out of the garage and tell him Gerard is sick," Mom ordered as she hurried to the phone in her bedroom.

I walked downstairs and into the garage. It was a fever; he wasn't deathly ill for crying out loud!

I peeked in at Dad tinkering at his tool bench while he listened to the Doors.

"Yo. Dad. Mom wants you. Gerard is sick or something," I said.

"Okay, be up in a minute," he said as he turned his radio off and put away a few manly things I didn't know the names of.

"Let's see how your brother is doing." He squeezed my shoulders and walked back into the house.

We walked upstairs together and heard the sound of bathwater running.

Dad opened the bathroom door. "What's up? Stef said G is sick."

"Yes! I need to bring this temperature down; it's 105! I just gave him Motrin, but Dr. Browne said I should give him a tepid bath, too." Mom's voice cracked.

My dad put his arm around her. "It's just a fever. He'll be okay."

Dad retrieved Gerard out of his crib and handed him to Mom.

"Do you mind just warming up the leftover spaghetti from last night, Simon? I am wiped," Mom asked in a very tired voice. She placed Gerard in the tub. He wasn't as smiley as usual. He must be feeling sick.

"That's what microwaves are for," Dad replied. "Come on, Stef. You can help me make the garlic bread."

Dad and I went to the kitchen. It didn't look as spotless as usual. Mom couldn't stand having the kitchen dirty, but there were crumbs on the granite countertops and a cabinet open.

Dad didn't seem to notice, so I let the crumbs hang out on the counter while he preheated the oven. I searched the pantry for the French bread. I grabbed it and set it on the crumby counter. I didn't really mind making the garlic bread, because I loved eating it. My dad sliced the bread in halves, and I buttered it. I placed chopped garlic cloves over the top.

"Cheese?" I looked up at Dad.

"Extra cheese!" Dad handed me shredded mozzarella. I sprinkled it on top of the sliced bread.

"Put her in," Dad said.

He put the bowl of spaghetti in the microwave while I placed the cookie sheet with bread into the oven. Ten minutes should do it.

When the bread was done, Dad cut it into slices and we sat at the round kitchen table. It was so quiet without Gerard at his high chair.

"So, tell me again how much Lakeside loved us," my dad smirked as he chewed his garlic bread. A string of mozzarella stuck in his goatee.

"They loved Quandary, Dad, but they were wondering why the guitarist was saving food in his beard for later," I giggled. I felt a little better after Mom and I talked, even with Gerard's rude interruption.

Dad's tongue grazed his beard until he found the stringy cheese. He slurped it into his mouth.

"Appetizing," I said. "So, how in the world did you get to play at our school?"

"Well," Dad answered. "Gina works with someone on the PTO at the insurance agency. Her friend saw us play one night and suggested that we play after the state testing. Of course, this was after we said we'd play for free."

"I can't believe you guys didn't tell me!" I said again.

"I thought it would be fun to surprise you, Stef," he answered. "If I'd known you were going country, I'd have learned a new Luke Bryan song for ya."

"Ha, ha. Very funny." I stuck my tongue out at him, then smiled.

We finished our spaghetti, and Dad left Mom's plate on the counter. He put the dishes in the dishwasher. He must feel bad for Mom, because he usually just leaves them in the sink.

"Did you practice your piano yet today?" he asked.

"Nope," I flinched. "I was just about to!"

"Let's get twenty minutes in, Stef. Your lessons aren't free you know," Dad said with a serious look on his face.

What happened to fun Dad? I suppose he's worried about Gerard, too.

As I placed my songbook on the piano, Dad headed up the stairs. I heard him tell Mom that he'd rock Gerard in the glider so she could eat.

My black piano was a hand-me-down from my Grandma Jo. She moved into an apartment and didn't have room for it. I was excited when we first got it, because I loved to pound on the keys, but my mom had other plans for it. I had to learn actual songs and press the keys gently.

Now I didn't love the piano. It wasn't too bad, but I wanted to play guitar like my Dad. He and my mom said I couldn't play guitar until I took piano lessons for two years. It was my second year, so next year I could finally take guitar lessons and get a guitar. I already had my eye on a black-and-white striped one at the music store where my lessons were.

I flipped to "Moonlight Sonata" and clumsily played it. I actually could play pretty well, but tonight I just wasn't into it.

Mom called from the kitchen, "Stef, you can do better than that."

Everyone's a critic. I concentrated harder and played the song a few times more. I couldn't let my parents think I wasn't responsible enough to play guitar. After exactly twenty minutes, I stopped midsong. I mean, my dad did say twenty minutes.

I crept up the stairs so my mom wouldn't make me play any longer. I closed the door to my bedroom and sat on my bed with my laptop. It was a Christmas gift from my grandparents. I figured I'd watch some music videos on YouTube on my computer. I'd heard that the Foo Fighters' new video was hilarious. I watched it four times in a row, because it was ridiculously funny.

I peeked out my door and said, "Dad, you have to see this!" Mom was just coming up the stairs from the kitchen. Dad handed her a flushed-looking Gerard, and she took over the rocking duty. She started singing, "Hey, baby," softly to him. She used to sing that same No Doubt song to me when I was little.

I played the video for Dad at my desk. People occasionally told him that he looked like the lead singer from Foo Fighters, except of course his hair is short because of his job. I think it's just because they are both middle-aged goofballs with toothy smiles and play guitar.

My dad remarked, "That Dave guy is one handsome dude."

I laughed. He always says that after someone tells him that he looks like the Foo Fighters guy.

"I'm going down to watch the game, Stef. Do you have homework?"

"Oh, yeah," I stammered. "Just a few questions." I retrieved my social studies book off the cluttered floor and my secret stash of Smarties from a shoebox in my closet. I crunched the tasty candies and finished the last two questions at my desk. I liked to think that Smarties made me finish my schoolwork faster.

I then went back to my laptop and searched for some tunes from this new band I'd heard on the radio. I loved how music could let you escape. I was halfway through my second video when I heard Mom shriek.

I set my laptop on my dresser and ran into Gerard's room. Mom hovered over the crib and was moaning, "Oh, no! Simon! Come quick."

I looked at Gerard. He looked different. His left arm was stiff and his body was shaking oddly. Oh my God. His eyes were rolled back. What was wrong with him?

Mom turned and looked at me with tears streaming down her cheeks. "Stef, get your dad. Now!"

"Oh, Gerard," I heard Mom weep.

I ran down the stairs and yelled, "Dad!" He was in the kitchen peering into the refrigerator.

"It's Gerard" is all I said. My face must've shown the seriousness of the situation.

Dad ran upstairs without closing the refrigerator door. I shut it and ran up after him.

Dad stepped into Gerard's room. "Stef, you stay in your room. I don't want you to see this," he said frantically.

I would normally have been put irritated by this, but I was worried. Really worried.

Chapter Eighteen

Dad ran to their bedroom and grabbed the phone. I stood in the doorway of my room and watched him press three numbers. My heart was pounding. Dad was pacing up a storm. I felt like I was in a movie.

"I need an ambulance! My baby boy is seizing. Yes. This is Simon Lucas. 120 Birch Street. Yes. 105. Do you think? Okay. Thank you." My dad dropped the phone on the bed and ran back into Gerard's room.

I sat down on my bed, my head spinning. "Please be okay," I prayed. "Please let Gerard be okay."

I stopped breathing so I could hear my dad talking to my mom.

"It could be a febrile seizure, honey. That's what the dispatcher thought due to his fever. He will be okay. He will."

My mom kept saying, "It's okay, Gerard. Mama's here. You'll be fine." I could tell she was still crying.

I heard Lyric whining softly in Gerard's room.

After about a minute, Dad yelled, "He stopped. He stopped."

Oh my God. Did he stop breathing?

Mom started sobbing harder than ever.

Oh my God, no. He can't be…

"Is Gerard okay?" I rushed into the room. I think my heart stopped beating.

"Honey, he stopped convulsing. I think that's a good sign," Dad choked out.

He hugged me, and I wiped tears of relief off my face.

My mom rubbed Gerard's arm. Her brown eyes were wet, and the creases around her eyes seemed even deeper if that was possible. She pulled me in for a hug. I buried my face into her damp shoulder.

We heard the sirens' ominous wailing and glanced at the window. While my dad opened the shade, I looked at the clock. Four minutes. It'd only been four minutes since Dad called. It seemed like twenty.

Dad brushed past me as he ran downstairs to open the front door.

"Honey, can you go to your room so the paramedics have room in here?" my mom asked.

I sat on my bed. I listened to Dad open up the door for the paramedics.

The next ten minutes were a blur. Two emergency medical technicians rushed into Gerard's room. They were armed with kits with all kinds of medical equipment. I peeked in to watch them take

Gerard's pulse. He whimpered a little then fell asleep.

I tried to listen in on the hushed voices of the adults as I curled up on my bed. I felt sick to my stomach. I'd been so mean to Gerard, and he was just a baby, my brother, my own flesh and blood. I had even wished he was never born! He had to be okay. He just had to be.

The paramedics reassured my mom and suggested she take him to the emergency room tonight or the family doctor tomorrow morning for a re-check.

After the paramedics left, I hugged my mom again. She looked so lost. My dad hugged us both and said, "Stef, everything's okay. Go brush your teeth and go to bed."

I nodded and did just that. I tossed and turned so much that Lyric left my side after ten minutes. She usually snuggled right next to my legs every night. She went and slept next to Gerard's crib.

Lyric was probably watching the baby to make sure he was okay. I laid still in my bed so I could hear if Gerard was okay. I checked the glowing clock every five minutes. The last time I looked at the clock it was 12:12. I finally fell asleep.

Chapter Nineteen

My alarm went off at 6:32 playing the usual song, "Beautiful Day" by U2. My mom programmed it to play it each time the alarm went off. She said this song would start each day with positive vibes. I was positive I was tired and hit snooze. I had not slept well. I kept thinking about Gerard convulsing. I even went into Gerard's room at 3:30 a.m. to check on him. Lyric was snuggled on the floor with my mom. At least Mom had brought her pillow and blanket. That couldn't be too comfy sleeping on the floor.

Six minutes later U2 came on again. I had to get up for school. It was a half day, so maybe I could nap when I got home. I forced myself out of bed and gathered my hair into a ponytail.

I peeked into Gerard's room. Mom was asleep. Gerard was breathing steadily. Lyric lifted her head up and thumped her tail on the carpet when she saw me, but then she placed her head on my mom's leg. She closed her eyes. It was a long night for everyone.

I heard Dad filling the coffee pot downstairs. He's usually the first one up. I tiptoed down the stairs and gave him a hug.

"You look like you got as much sleep as the rest of us," he yawned.

"Do you think Gerard will be okay?" I asked.

"Yes. I really do, Stef. You let Mom and I worry about him, and you worry about school," he answered. Hopefully honestly.

He tousled my hair and sat in his navy boxer briefs at the kitchen table, eating his English muffin with peanut butter on it. I think I'm the only modest member of the Lucas family. My mom walks on the treadmill in a t-shirt and undies. Gerard is just in a diaper half the time. Thankfully Dad remembers to put pajama pants on when I have friends sleep over. That would be embarrassing if they saw my parents in their underwear. I've already had enough embarrassing undies moments in my life, thank you.

I poured myself some orange juice and stood and ate my English muffin with butter that Dad made me.

"Have a seat, Stef, and eat," Dad reminded me. "You know Mom hates when you walk around and eat. Crumbs get all over."

Lyric slinked into the room and looked up at me in anticipation of any crumbs falling toward her. Poor girl, Mom has all these cleanliness rules. Lyric hardly ever gets any table scraps. That will change when Gerard starts eating more solid foods.

103

I sat with Dad who took the last bite of his muffin and licked his fingers. He had peanut butter stuck in his moustache.

"Ewww, Dad," I said, handing him a cloth napkin. "Could you please keep the food in your mouth?"

He wiped his mouth and threw the napkin at me.

I started to yell at him, but he put his finger to his lips. Oh, yeah. I probably shouldn't wake Gerard and Mom.

"Gotta get movin' so I can be home in time for band practice tonight," he said as he put his dishes in the sink.

"Gabi's sleeping over," I said. Then I wondered if she could still come after Gerard's episode last night. "Do you think it's okay if she still comes?"

"I'll talk with Mom about it, Stef. She's been through the wringer." He headed upstairs to shower.

Gerard was going to ruin my plans yet again.

I felt a pang of guilt in my stomach. I'm such a terrible big sister. I climbed the stairs to get ready for my day.

When I sat down on the bus, Gabi asked me right away if everything was okay. How could she know already that I'd had a rough night?

I huddled with her on the bus and told her about Gerard. I just didn't feel like broadcasting the news to everyone. I didn't want to have to explain it over and over. It was awful enough just describing the convulsions to Gabi.

"That poor sweet baby!" Gabi whispered. Tears sprang to her eyes, which made tears well up in my own.

I willed my tears to stay in my eyes and said, "My dad thinks he should be fine. He mentioned something about a febrile seizure. I'll have to google it after school today."

"At least it's a half day," Gabi said.

I nodded and closed my eyes. My head rested on the back of the seat until we got to school. I was exhausted.

Gabi and I walked to our lockers. Despite my eventful week, I wasn't in the mood to really talk to anyone but Gabi today. Brooke waved to me; I just gave her a half smile. That's all I could do. I noticed she was wearing a black skirt with a bright turquoise blue top. At least she wasn't a replica of Gina today. Then I looked at myself in my locker mirror. I did look tired. My hair was in a haphazard, frizzy ponytail, and I had dark circles under my eyes. I even had jeans on that I'd worn on Wednesday and just picked off the floor of my closet. I looked at my black Swatch. Almost four hours to go until I could go home and take a nap. I should probably brush my teeth too. I realized I'd forgotten to when I licked my front teeth. They were a little fuzzy.

"Do you have any gum?" I asked Gabi. She handed me a square piece of peppermint gum from her heart-shaped purse. Gabi owned about ten purses. I didn't have one purse yet. I figured it would be one more thing to keep track of. I just kept everything in my backpack. And when I did get one, it wasn't going to have a picture of Ross Lynch from the Disney Channel on it. Gabi never mentioned any boys at school, but she had a huge crush on Ross. We must have seen every episode of his TV show at least ten times.

I quickly chewed the fresh-tasting gum on the way to class. Mrs. Stark didn't allow gum in class, so I tossed it into the garbage before I sat at my desk. I made it through the day robotically going through the motions of the mindless tasks my teacher gave me. It wasn't until just before chorus that I finally woke up.

Jenna and I walked in the hallway together as we always did. She chattered away about something, and I just said, "Uh, huh" and "No kidding" a few times so she thought I was listening. Then she said in mid-sentence, "There's Charlie!"

"How do I look?" she frantically asked me as she squeezed my wrist. She looked good as usual, and I told her so. Then just as I noticed Josh walking with Charlie, I remembered I wasn't looking so hot today.

Josh and Charlie strutted along as cool seventh graders do, and both looked at us just before we passed them.

"'Sup?" Josh said as he looked at me.

Jenna squealed, "Hi, guys! Great!" I noticed that she swung her hips back and forth more pronounced as the boys went by. Maybe Josh was talking to Jenna and not me.

Jenna turned to me again. "I didn't know you knew Josh. Maybe you could talk to him about Charlie for me!"

Maybe Josh had spoken to me after all! I squealed inside my head, and then composed myself and said, "He used to ride my bus, but I don't know him that well."

A big grin then slipped out. Jenna grinned back. Maybe she did know I thought he was the cutest boy in school.

Jenna and I floated into chorus.

"What are you two grinning about?" Skyler asked as we sat down.

"Oh, nothing," Jenna said as she gave me a sideways glance.

"What is up with your hair today, Stef?" Skyler went on. She was always good for a dig or two during chorus.

I fluffed my frizzy ponytail and sighed. I was too tired to make a witty retort.

A young, blond substitute teacher rang the triangle to start the class. She must have been just out of college. She looked more like she was in high school, and she acted like she was nervous.

The class sensed her fear and didn't quiet down for her. The substitute cracked her gum and put her hands on her hips. She rang the triangle again. When Miss Lee did that, the class quieted right away. No such luck for Miss Newbie.

Miss Newbie wrote her name on the board with pink chalk. Her name was Miss Tarkin. She even dotted her "i" with a heart. She picked something up from the shelf, turned around, and yelled, "Silencio!" as she swung a conductor's baton in the air at us.

I don't know if she thought we'd think it was cool that she read Harry Potter or if she really thought it was a magic wand. But she was no Hermione Granger, because no one was silenced. In fact, Skyler busted out laughing and everyone followed suit. Even me. The laughter was contagious, and this teacher was ridiculous.

Mike yelled, "Expelliarmus!" which made the class laugh even harder. Miss Tarkin's face scrunched up and she grabbed a pen and a tablet of paper off Miss Lee's desk.

She walked up to Mike and said, "Here's a behavior slip for your obnoxious behavior."

He cussed under his breath, but said nothing else. Well, a behavior slip is much more powerful than a conductor's baton, and finally the class was silenced.

Miss Tarkin smiled in a fake way and said, "If anyone else wants to be rude to an authority figure like myself, you will be given a behavior slip, too."

She handed out worksheets on the history of jazz. I wished Miss Lee was here. She never had us do boring worksheets.

Miss Tarkin then put a CD in. She said that if it was up to her, she'd be playing a Beyonce CD, but Miss Lee wanted the class to be exposed to jazz. She pressed play.

Trumpets sounded and a jazz band played something with lyrics about summertime.

A few students swayed to the music while reading the paragraph about jazz.

Skyler nudged me and said, "This is the smoothest jazz I've ever heard. But you prefer frizzy, right?" and she pointed to my ponytail.

I really didn't have the patience for this anymore.

"Shut it, Skyler!" I said. I didn't yell, but it wasn't exactly an inside voice. And it so wasn't worth what happened next.

"You two girls, up front!" Miss Tarkin demanded.

She handed us each a slip. "You two have already been warned and now may take a trip to the dean's office. You can join them, too, Mike."

Perfect. I'd never been to the dean's office ever.

I protested, "But! It was just…"

"Too bad, so sad," Miss Tarkin said and pointed to the door. The three of us plodded to the dean's office with our heads down in defeat.

Chapter Twenty

Mr. Brennen nodded to the three wooden chairs in his office. We sat down obediently.

He looked through the behavior slips quickly and asked us why we were here.

I wanted to say, "Didn't you just read why we were here?" but I stopped myself.

Mike said, "Sorry. I guess we were rude to the substitute. I won't get detention again, will I Mr. Brennen?"

You could say that Mike is the class clown who has had a few behavior slips before. He was pretty funny, which is why he sometimes got away with it, but sometimes a teacher had no choice but to give him a slip so others wouldn't act out.

Mr. Brennen patted Mike on the shoulder. "Let's just talk this out and see. Tell me what happened."

Mike told him about the conductor's wand and what Miss Tarkin yelled and then what he yelled. Mr. Brennen tried not to smile.

"Okay, why are you girls in here?"

Skyler actually looked a little scared. She wrung her hands in her lap and didn't look up at anyone. I thought she always kept her cool.

"Can I talk to you in private for a minute?" I asked Mr. Brennan in my most polite voice.

Skyler looked up quizzically, and Mr. Brennen asked the other two to step out of his office for a moment.

"What is it, Stefani?" he asked.

"I know what I did was wrong. I yelled during class at Skyler who was teasing me. I know I should just ignore it, but I had a really hard night." I looked up at him. I could feel tears start to form in my eyes.

Mr. Brennen looked at me with genuine concern, "Go on."

"My baby brother had a seizure last night and the ambulance came and I hardly slept and I'm really worried about him," I blurted out. A tear escaped, but I brushed it away so Mr. Brennen wouldn't see.

"I see. I'm so sorry to hear that, Stefani." He patted my shoulder. "The buses will be leaving soon anyway, and since this isn't normal behavior for you to act out, I'll give you a break. I think you've had a hard enough day."

I smiled gratefully at him. "What about the other two?"

Mr. Brennen ripped up the behavior slips. "Just between you and me, I'm not sure I can take these seriously when there are hearts dotting the i's."

He opened the door and asked the others to come in.

"You are dismissed. No slips for today, but in the future please be more respectful to our substitute teachers. Get to your lockers, the bell is about to ring."

"Yessss," Mike said with his fist in the air.

We walked to the sixth-grade lockers together through the empty halls.

"What did you say to Mr. Brennen?" Skyler asked.

"I just explained that it had been a rough week, and I wouldn't do it again."

Skyler said in a quiet voice, "Sorry, Stef, for making fun of you."

I was glad that she said sorry, but I knew and she knew it wouldn't be her last bout of teasing.

"I guess Miss Tarkin was mistaken. We aren't going to get into trouble after all!" Mike whooped to Skyler and me.

We laughed. It felt good to laugh and release some of my tension.

The bell rang and the hordes of middle school students rushed to their lockers to get home for the weekend. TGIF indeed.

On the bus, I gave Gabi a quick rundown about the chorus situation. I didn't want to tell her that I'd cried in the dean's office, but we did giggle over Miss Tarkin. I wondered if she was going to substitute teach at Lakeside again.

The bus slowed to my stop. I realized that I'd never asked my mom if Gabi could still come over.

"I'll text you!" I yelled to Gabi as I got off the bus.

The front door was locked so I got in through the garage door. We had a secret code that we could punch in and the garage door would open. Both cars were gone. Where was Mom?

I walked into the kitchen, and the breakfast dishes were still in the sink. Gerard's high chair had baby food on it. Lyric bounded up for me to pat her head. She was here, but where in the world were Mom and the baby?

My heart sunk. Maybe Gerard had another seizure. Maybe Mom just took him to the doctor. Or maybe he was in the hospital!

I ran to the phone and dialed my mom's cell number.

"Home Sweet Home" by Mötley Crüe came from the top of the microwave. Mom's phone. That was her ring tone for when someone called her from home. I couldn't believe she forgot her phone.

I opened and closed the phone so it would stop singing. My stomach growled and I realized I needed to have lunch. I wasn't hungry this morning and had only had a half of a banana.

Even though I was worried, I figured an empty stomach wasn't going to do me any good. I

114

slapped two pieces of wheat bread on a plate and got out the ham and Swiss cheese.

I slumped into my chair with my chocolate milk and sandwich, then I heard the door to the garage open.

I dropped my sandwich and ran to meet Mom. She was carrying Gerard. He was smiling and remarkably, so was Mom.

"Hi, honey." She kissed my forehead. "How was your day?"

"Me? How is Gerard? Where were you?" I was exasperated. I extracted my hair out of Gerard's grasp. At least he didn't mind frizzy.

"We went to see Dr. Browne. She looked Gerard over and said it was most likely a febrile seizure like the paramedics said. Luckily since he's a baby, we'll have him on a monitor so we'll hear if it happens again. It could happen or not. We just don't know. If it does, we'll have to take him to a pediatric neurologist. We just hope it doesn't come to that."

She kissed Gerard's head and put him down on the kitchen tile. She poured herself a glass of water.

"Thankfully Gerard no longer has a fever. So I am certainly glad about that," Mom said after a sip of water.

"I was so worried," I said, and I hugged Mom.

She gave me a giant squeeze back. I looked up to her and noticed she had some frizzy hair going on too.

"I think it will be all right, Stef. These seizures are more common than we think. And Gerard may never have one again. Which I pray and hope he doesn't." She picked up Gerard again. She held Gerard out to me as if to give him to me, but then pulled him back.

"Mom, I'll hold him so you can make a sandwich," I said. I kissed my baby brother on his chubby cheek. He giggled.

"Thanks, honey. We are all exhausted. How about after lunch, we'll all take a nap when Gerard does."

"Definitely!" I said. I couldn't wait to crawl into my comfy bed.

As we ate lunch, I decided to bring up Gabi's sleepover.

"Believe it or not, Quandary is still coming over because there is no other place to practice." She rolled her eyes. Then she smiled, "What's one more person?"

"Thanks, Mom!" I texted Gabi to tell her the good news. Then I fell into the comfiest bed in the world. At least it was that afternoon.

Chapter Twenty-one

I played with Gerard on the floor while Mom washed the dishes from dinner. He couldn't help being so cute. He rocked back and forth on his knees. Mom said he would be crawling any day now. Mom explained that she'd really have to be on her toes once he was moving. I understood, and I was okay with that.

The annoying clock on the mantel chimed six times. Gabi couldn't come over until after her dance class, but should be here soon for our sleepover. I laid down on the floor and let Gerard grab my nose. He was amused by such simple things.

I absentmindedly patted my full stomach. Too much chicken tetrazzini. Then I admired my black nails. Mom had painted them after our nap. They looked pretty darn cool and matched my black Quandary t-shirt that Mom had made for me.

The doorbell rang.

"Finally!" I said as I ran to the foyer and swung the door open.

"Hey, Stef!" Gabi called to me.

We walked into the family room where Gerard was laying on a blanket on the carpet, tugging at Lyric's pull toy. Gerard tugged at the toy, and then Lyric tugged it back ever so gently with her teeth. Gerard giggled. Lyric was always more gentle with Gerard. I told you, she's a smart dog.

"That is so cute!" Gabi exclaimed.

"I know," I agreed. I picked up Gerard and gave the green toy to the dog. Gerard whined a little, but Lyric happily thumped her tail. I blew on Gerard's belly until he forgot about the toy.

"Mom, here's the baby." I handed her Gerard in the kitchen.

"Thanks for watching him, Stef, so I could finish the dishes. Oh, hey, Gabi!"

"Hi, Mrs. Lucas," Gabi chirped.

I grabbed her pillow, and we brought her things up to my room.

Gabi opened my closet to put her overnight bag in there and pulled out my dance trophy.

"Why in the world is this in the closet? I would have loved to win this," she scolded.

"It's embarrassing, that's why. If it was a headbanging trophy, it would be displayed on the mantel in our family room!"

"Stef! I am putting it on your shelf with the Neon Trees drumstick and the picture of your dad with Mötley Crüe."

"Noooo!" I laughed, but I let her put it up there. I could always store guitar picks in the cup. My dad always gives them to me if he catches one at the concerts he goes to.

"Gina will be here any minute," I told her.

We listened to music and giggled over the strange week.

"Can you believe Skyler got in trouble from her mom for wearing so much black eyeliner to school?" asked Gabi.

"I know!" I replied. "Who does she think she is? Lady Gaga?"

Gabi cracked up. "At least things seemed almost back to normal today," Gabi said. "You were in a black t-shirt and the other girls were wearing their regular clothes."

"Yeah," I said. "But I did wear a red belt and bracelet. I guess a little color doesn't hurt. And no one had to use the Heimlich the rest of the week."

"That was crazy. I'm so relieved that Josh was okay," Gabi said.

"Yeah, who else would I sneak looks at in the hall if he wasn't," I said.

Gabi giggled, "Well, Dakota is kind of cute…"

"What?!" I shrieked. Gabi never said any boy in school was cute ever!

"Girls, come on down!" my mom called.

Gina was at the front door.

"Hey, Gina!" I ran to her and gave her a hug.

"Hi, Stef. Nice shirt," Gina said.

"Thanks," I replied with a big smile.

Gabi tugged at me.

"Gina, this is my friend, Gabi."

"Hey, Gabi! I saw you sitting next to Stef during our concert."

"Hi, Gina," Gabi said shyly. "Quandary was awesome!"

"Yeah, and you were quite the hero," I said to Gina.

Gina shook her head and said, "I am just glad that boy was okay. That was scary."

My mom said, "We're proud of you! You did some quick thinking."

Gina smiled, "You would have done the same thing if you were in my situation. I'm sure of it. And you had your fair share of medical excitement here, too."

Gerard reached over and grabbed Gina's hair.

"Hey!" Gina exclaimed. "There's my little cutie, baby G!"

Gina grabbed Gerard out of my mom's arms, and she and my mom walked upstairs to put him to bed.

"I'm so glad you are feeling better," Gina cooed to Gerard.

"Girls, I air-popped some popcorn. It's on the counter," my mom called to us.

We grabbed some water bottles and the popcorn bowl and walked downstairs to the basement.

Our basement wasn't finished yet. Half of the basement was filled with boxes and containers for storage. The other half was set up with instruments on a red carpet remnant for band practice. My dad had decorated the cement walls with band posters. He had been collecting them since he was a teenager…everyone from the Beatles and Ozzy Osbourne to Papa Roach and Avenged Sevenfold. I think we had over twenty posters. And not any One Direction posters like Gabi had taped up all over her room.

Chapter Twenty-two

"Quandary is in the house!" my dad yelled as I jumped off the last step. Jack and my dad started warming up. It sounded like an Evanescence song. A few months ago I requested that they sing a few Evanescence songs. Gina can really belt them out.

My mom and Gina came down into the basement. Mom placed the baby monitor on the shelf by the door.

Mom smiled at me and said, "Gerard is asleep. I can finally sit down." She sat down on a folding chair. "I'm still nervous though about the whole seizure thing. So I'll be up and down checking on him between songs."

My dad rubbed her back.

"Well, don't leave yet," my dad said. "Do you want to hear the new song I've been working on?"

"Sweet. I can't wait to try it out," Gina said. Mom tiredly nodded.

He handed Gina a piece of paper with the lyrics on it.

"Cool title. "Rock 'n' Roll Princess!'" Gina said.

"I wrote it for my girls," my dad said, looking at my mom then me.

My mom beamed. My cheeks warmed.

"Well, let's hear it," I said, rubbing my neck.

"1,2,3,4," Jack said, and my dad started playing the guitar.

My dad sang the words with Gina since it was brand new for her.

Mom, Gabi, and I bounced to the music.

"Because she's my rock 'n' roll princess, yeah," Gina sang. Dad jumped up as he played the final note.

Mom, Gabi, and I clapped wildly. It was a great tune, and best of all, he wrote it for Mom and me.

Gabi yelled, "Woo hoo!"

I laughed, because she's always "Woo-hooing."

"Killer song, Dad!" I yelled to him.

Dad bowed, and the band started up again with a 30 Seconds to Mars song.

Gabi and I danced to the next three songs.

Gabi turned and bowed to me. "Ready, pardner?"

I giggled, curtsied back and took her hand. We do-si-doed and did the square dance routine from gym class.

After the song, my dad yelled, "Yee haw! Congrats to the square dance champion of Lakeside

Middle School! Who knew my little rocker knew how to do the two-step?"

It wasn't the two-step – my dad knows nothing about country music -- but Gabi and I curtsied and bowed to the band and Mom.

Then the band took a short break. My mom dashed upstairs to check on Gerard. I walked to Gina to show her my dark nails and the bottle of black nail polish.

"Very cool, Stef!" she said approvingly. "Hey, look at my toes."

Gina slipped off her right Tom's shoe and pulled out her foot.

"Your toenails are painted black!" I exclaimed. I couldn't stop my big smile, because Gina had the same idea as me.

"Awesome," Gabi said.

"Maybe I'll do my fingernails for the next concert," Gina said to us. "I'm parched. I'm going to grab an ice water. Do you girls need anything?"

"Nope!" I said.

"I'm good," Gabi said. Gina walked up the stairs as my mom walked down.

Gabi turned to me and said, "Your cousin is so cool."

"Yeah, she's the best," I said. "I have an idea! I'll paint your nails, Gabi." I pulled her to the chair.

I took the black nail polish out of my pocket and started painting Gabi's nails. Gabi gasped and looked horrified. She pulled her hand away.

"What? You don't like it?" I asked.

"Well. Not so much," she sheepishly said.

She rubbed the black off her nails with a napkin.

"I have a light pink that will go well with your skirt, Gabi," my mom suggested. My mom left to go get the nail polish.

"Thanks, Mrs. Lucas," said Gabi.

"Sorry about that, Gabi," I said to my best friend. "Like the song says, you should just be yourself."

She snorted as she tried to stifle her laugh, and then we both burst out laughing.

We were just being ourselves.

If you enjoyed this book by this author,
please consider leaving a review at
your favorite retailer or on Goodreads!

ACKNOWLEDGEMENTS

First, thank you to my readers. Thank you for reading my story about Stef. I hope I made you smile, giggle, or even tear up a little. Don't forget that kindness is easier than you think. You rock!

Thank you to my wonderful beta readers and critiquers (I hope I didn't forget anyone!). Hugs and thank you's to my bff Becky Monroe and her daughter Abby, and also my daughter Em for catching some obvious mistakes! Thank you to my local writing group who guided me from near and afar: Angela Scaperlanda Bujan, Cathy Ralston, and Ann Bryson. An extra HUGE thank you to Cathy for her fabulous editing skills!

I love the online writing community! Thank you so much to all of you for your support and friendship. I really enjoy the interactions on our blogs, Twitter and Facebook. So fun going on this writing journey together. Especially thank you to the following amazing people who gave me suggestions for this book: Anita M, Carolina VM, Tina L, Marcia H, Hema P, Sharon M, Marietta, Jude, Terrie, and Mark M.

A hurrah and thank you to Tom Maple for the cover photo and Steven Novak for the amazing cover design.

Thank you also to my wonderful family and friends who RT on Twitter, spread the word on

Facebook about my books and like my posts. You make me smile. Big Smile!

Thank you to my fave bands who rejuvenate me during live concerts and keep me going on my chauffeuring trips and on the treadmill. Many of my favorite bands are mentioned in this book. Check them out. It's only rock 'n' roll, but I love it.

Lastly, thank you to my family. Thank you to my parents Trudy, Tom and Mary, my sister Denise, my in-laws Bobbi and Roger, my husband Chris, my three fabulous kids – Josh, Em, and Jack. Family is everything. Thank you for being my cheerleaders and support system! Thanks to God for all of his blessings.

READING ROCKS!
♫